Awakening

Awakening

DEVON SCOTT

Kensington Publishing Corp.
http://www.kensingtonbooks.com

DAFINA BOOKS are published by

Kensington Publishing Corp.
119 West 40th Street
New York, NY 10018

Copyright © 2002 by Devon Scott
Published in arrangement with Strebor Books, P.O. Box 1370 Bowie, MD 20718.
http://www.streborbooks.com.
Distributed by Simon & Schuster, Inc., 1230 Avenue of the Americas, New York, NY 10020. 1-800-223-2336.
Jasminium © 2002 by Jonathan Luckett
ISBN 1-59309-007-2. LCCN 2003105024
First Printing: November 2003

All Kensington Titles, Imprints, and Distributed Lines are available at special quantity discounts for bulk purchases for sales promotion, premiums, fund-raising, educational, or institutional use. Special book excerpts or customized printings can also be created to fit specific needs. For details, write or phone the office of the Kensington special sales manager: Kensington Publishing Corp., 119 West 40th Street, New York, NY 10018, attn: Special Sales Department, Phone: 1-800- 221-2647.

Dafina and the Dafina logo Reg. U.S. Pat. & TM Off.

ISBN-13: 978-1-4967-0242-5
ISBN-10: 1-4967-0242-5
First Kensington Mass Market Edition: July 2016

10   9   8   7   6   5   4   3   2   1

Printed in the United States of America

Prologue

There is an ancient Ethiopian proverb, one that has been handed down from generation to generation, that loosely translated means, "when one's eyes quiver . . ." Depending on which eye does the quivering—either the person is going to receive bad news and cry, or they will encounter someone they haven't seen in an incredibly long time . . . One thing is indeed clear—Ethiopians take this omen seriously—and pay close attention to the quivering of one's eyes—for one way or another, something unforeseen and unexpected is bound to happen . . .

One

The snow drifts lazily to earth, the way leaves flutter to the ground caught in an autumn breeze, descending in a haphazard fashion, see-sawing back and forth, each oversized, water-laden snowflake following its own course immune to the path of others. Taj presses his nose and cheek against the dual-pane window and exhales gently, observing his breath fan out across the sheet of cold glass before fading quickly, as if an aberration—a bubbling well in a sea of sand dunes. He glances down forty-something stories to the Manhattan street below, which one he isn't exactly sure; they are staying at the *W* hotel at Times Square—it could be West 47th or Eighth Avenue. Taj never has possessed a keen sense of direction. One thing is clear: it isn't Broadway that he is staring at. He is certain of that.

Taj presses his cheek again to the glass. The cold feels good on his smooth dark skin. He glances upward, marveling as he does each time he returns to the city at the diversity of structures and their architectures—like the city itself, a microcosm of multiplicity—granite, steel, brick, aluminum, old and new in peaceful coexistence, like hip-hop and jazz. He never grows tired of exploring her structures—the details, fine lines, and craftsmanship that speak to him of art, creativity, and a way of constructing things long since retired. He subscribes to this mode of thinking, this way of life.

"These are some big-ass snowflakes," Taj remarks softly. He turns slightly, taking in the brown couch, low coffee table, wall unit, and entrance to the bedroom. A single lamp by the couch is illuminated. Soft music emanates from the clock radio in the bedroom. The two-room suite is small, yet comfortable. Perhaps the mood has something to do with the snow—the way hundreds of flakes each second collide with the tall windows, opening up, smearing their contents on the glass.

"Please. I hate it when you talk like that."

"Like what?" he asks, already knowing the answer as he turns toward her. He stares at Nicole. She is on the couch, her legs folded underneath her, shoes off, with thin square-frame glasses perched atop a perfectly shaped nose. Her dark eyes, enhanced by brown caramel skin and rosy cheeks, flick over to him briefly before turning quickly back to her book—a leafy hardback, James Baldwin no less.

"You know, trying to talk like that. 'Big-ass?' It doesn't become you." Taj runs a hand over his chocolate baldhead and smiles. He loves his woman. Precisely at such times he knows this with the certainty of a Swiss quartz timepiece—watching her the way he is just now, thinking to himself how lucky he is to have someone like her in his life. And so Taj sighs, captures her wink, and turns away. As he returns his stare to the window, glancing down once again at the street, the stream of traffic, and warmly dressed people, he feels a sudden urge to be out among them.

Taj and Nicole walk hand in hand (more accurately, glove in glove), the two of them bundled against the deepening cold. Nicole's wool ear warmers keep her head somewhat shielded; her red ski parka seems to attract snow the way a summer barbecue attracts mosquitoes. Taj wears a long dark wool overcoat, collar turned up, that reaches nearly to his ankles, and one of those Russian military-style hats that submarine captains wore during the second world war, with real fur that peeks out as if a squirrel or rabbit were seeking refuge underneath. The snow is swirling around them, attacking from all angles, getting into their nostrils and eyes, pelting their heads and thighs. Nicole reaches for Taj's arm and intertwines hers with his, enjoying as they always do the closeness—the warmth that can be felt even now, on this bitter, New York evening. It is eight p.m., several weeks until Christmas. The streets are lined with holiday lights, decorations, and shoppers: courageous souls like them who have braved the elements in search of a sale or last minute gift item or, in the case of Taj and Nicole, have a chance to walk in one of the greatest cities in the world (just ask anyone in Manhattan!), marvel at the architectures, take in a museum or two, or just enjoy the magic and romance of this snow-covered evening.

The sound of music is everywhere, emanating from speakers hung on lampposts every hundred feet. Christmas favorites are cycled, ones that they sang as children, and Nicole can't help but hum along as Taj points upward at the carved molding on the top edge of an Eighth Avenue apartment building or co-op. Intricate patterns carved in stone are interspersed with decorative corbels; eighteenth-century faces gaze downward. An unending sea of taxicabs glides along choking the entire avenue, and Taj notices that not a single one is unoccupied.

Going nowhere in particular, they turn right at the corner and dash into a coffee house, as much for relief from the cold as to get something to eat and drink. They settle into a high table by the window, amazingly vacant at this exact moment, after ordering a pair of lattes and jelly-filled pastries. Nicole removes her ear warmers, shakes the snow from her thick hair with a quick zig-zag movement of her neck, and attacks the pastry with her fingers, tearing at the flaky bread as though it were wrapping paper. She watches Taj closely, reaching out as he removes his hat and wiping the moisture from his smooth dark head with her hand. His eye begins to quiver—again; the third or fourth time today (that she's noticed), the lower eyelid trembling as if to its own eclectic beat. She passes her fingers over it to cease its movement. He catches her left wrist as she pulls back, brings it to his mouth, and gazes at the ring silently before kissing her fingers gingerly. Nicole blinks back tears and stares at Taj for a long time. Their eyes are unwavering before movement outside their window releases their concentration on each other.

Nicole is speaking about *Giovanni's Room*, Baldwin's acclaimed novel set in Paris in the 1950s—a young man grappling with his sexuality and the pain of choosing between a man and a woman, and how she intends to weave next week's reading into a discussion with her students on sexuality in literature. Taj listens intently, watching her eyes animate as she speaks of her work—associate professor of American literature at Howard—adding Baldwin to his already extensive to-do list.

Redressing in their coats, hats, and gloves, the two reemerge forty minutes later, appetites satisfied and freezing limbs thawed, ready to brave the elements once again. They cut across the street during a momentary lull in traffic, Nicole in tow as Taj heads for a brownstone with a lone sign in the shape of a saxophone, pulsing blue neon. They stand for a moment discerning the jazz that escapes, deciding whether or not they wish to check it out. In the end, they decide to move on, still warm and cozy from the coffee and pastry, feeling the night air, the temperature seemingly on the rise.

Onward . . . past Christmas lights and the serene nativity scenes in store-front windows, then on to the neon madness and excessiveness of Broadway. Taj just shakes his head, attempting to quickly calculate how much power is expended in this four-block radius on signage alone. He gives up, recognizing it is of little consequence to him or others.

AWAKENING

Back onto side streets where life seems to move at one notch back from normal—third gear instead of fourth—down tree-lined blocks whose canopies are blanketed with fresh snow. Past residential homes that sport fully decorated trees in their parlor windows, each one more beautiful than the previous, as if the whole spirit of Christmas has been reduced to a competitive sport. Taj and Nicole walk hand in hand, drawing it all in, like smoke, inhaling the scent and the vapors—the very essence of the city.

They come to a dark stone church on the corner of a busy intersection—a three-building structure that is out of place among the steel and aluminum skyscrapers that tower toward the heavens, their top floors obliterated by the falling snow. The church is eighteenth century, Gothic in its design, embellished with cathedral spires and thick wrought-iron gates. A crowd of onlookers stands on the stone steps leading to enormous oak doors that are held open as though they are wings or outstretched palms, the bright warm lights inside inviting. Song can be heard spilling out into the night—Christmas carolers singing "Silent Night." Nicole turns to Taj and grins. He leads her up the stairs, past the onlookers, and into the sanctity of the church's interior.

Inside it is warm. Nicole shakes off the snow and Taj respectfully removes his hat. The pews are intermittently filled with folks who have come to hear the choir sing. They are diverse: blacks, whites, Asians, Africans, young and old, each putting aside their cultural differences on this night to sing songs that toll of the night Jesus Christ was born.

Crowds of people gather at the rear end of the church, as if afraid to move closer to the singers, or still deciding whether to stay or go. Taj leads Nicole past the throng, thick coats and jackets covered with melting snow that runs down the fabric and pools at their feet. Inching closer, Nicole behind him, his hand clasped in hers, fingers intertwined, they move past folks who have joined in with the carolers singing "O Holy Night," the sweet sound reverberating off of domed ceilings and stained glass windows. And then, as Taj is consumed by the sights, sounds, and smells within this church, his ears discern one strain that is unique and stands alone—and he pivots to search for the source: a woman's voice—distinctive and hauntingly familiar—sensual in its smooth delivery, a soulful melody that interlaces itself amidst the choir's song. Taj turns, first 180 degrees, then in the opposite direction. Nicole senses the change in him, like a flame extinguished from a sudden change in pressure, and asks if everything is okay. Taj ignores her, not in a disrespectful way, but some things can only be dealt in a serial way, one at a time, in order of priority. And so, Taj gives *this* his full attention.

Before the first row of pews is a black couple facing forward, their backs to the others. The woman, with her thick twisting hair tied back and head moving to an unknown beat, is accompanied by a tall, bald gentleman wearing an expensive camelhair coat. Taj is certain this woman is the source of the familiar melodic strain. Taj moves parallel with them and turns, releasing Nicole's hand as he does, looking past the man and observing the woman in profile. He watches her as the words of the song waft from her lips. A tidal wave of recognition rises up and crashes onto him with a force that stops his heart cold.

Twenty years.

Can that be right?

Yes.

Twenty years.

His movements are now beyond his control. He is being choreographed and flows along, his mind outside of himself as he shifts closer to the couple. And then without conscious thought, Taj opens his mouth, leans in, and says softly, "Jazz, look into my eyes . . . focus only on my eyes . . ."

* * *

Cheyenne is raptured by the sound, the way this choir has come together and filled this holy space with their sweet voices. She raises her head to the vaulted ceiling overhead and closes her eyes, matching their words but with a melody all her own. When Cheyenne is singing, she is in her element—it is what she is passionate about, what moves her, what makes her blood course through her veins with a sudden rush. She spies her husband Malcolm quickly glancing at his Movado. Yes, she knows they need to watch the time—there's a CD release party later on that evening at one of the city's hottest clubs. Malcolm, record executive and producer *extraordinaire* and currently one of the hottest and most powerful forces in urban music today, needs to be there at precisely the right moment. Cheyenne knows this all too well, the routine repeated many times during the last year. Not that she's complaining. The life they lead is storybook, no two ways about it. And yet tonight, what is most important to her right now is completing this song, singing these words that take her to a special place—many, many years ago, before she grew up and when her mamma was still here.

She leans into Malcolm, rubs his arm as he turns to her and smiles. He loves to hear her sing. It brings him comfort and joy. And so he reaches for her, placing his arm around her waist as he flashes her a smile, and he reminds her that they need to be going soon. Cheyenne silently nods.

"Jazz, look into my eyes . . ."

When she hears those words, uttered from behind her, the color drains from her face. Cheyenne ceases to sing. Her mind is racing, connecting thoughts with long-filed-away images.

" . . . Focus only on my eyes . . ."

She is already turning, a mixture of pain and pleasure filling her so quickly that she fears she will drown. And in an instant she is facing *him.* She raises her eyes slowly, as if not wanting the confirmation that is sure to come. But then their eyes meet, and she *knows.* One look at the eyes tells all. It's Taj.

"Oh–my–God," she mouths, so softly that no one, including her husband or Taj for that matter, can discern a single word. Tears freefall down her beautiful face. Never in a million years did she ever expect to see him again. And yet, staring into those amazing eyes, the ones she recalls with sudden clarity—hazel colored (the yin/yang of *that* color against his dark skin), their piercing yet calming intensity and almost magical qualities—Cheyenne is speechless. Suddenly, the air is being drawn out of this enormous room and she is finding it difficult to breathe. She is dizzy. Her husband turns back and flicks his stare between his wife and this stranger standing far too close.

"Baby?" he says, reaching for her. "Are you okay?"

Behind Taj, Nicole is watching the scene unfold. She hasn't heard the words that he spoke to this woman, but she has witnessed the reaction. Nicole, like Malcolm, has figured out (in the short time that has elapsed—five or six seconds) that something is not quite right.

Cheyenne continues to stare at Taj.

Taj silently returns her stare with his.

"Baby?" Malcolm says, louder this time as he turns to Taj. Malcolm and Taj are roughly the same size, Taj being a half-foot taller, but both possess similar characteristics—baldheads, dark-skinned complexions, and piercing stares.

Nicole reaches for her man, tugs at his shoulder as Cheyenne sobs louder. Taj waves Nicole off with a shrug and reaches for Cheyenne's face. He strokes it (cheek to chin with a single finger), smiles, and asks softly, "Have you remembered our pact, Jazz?"

Cheyenne opens her trembling mouth and responds, "Yes."

Taj smiles. "Good. I see life has treated you well." Cheyenne readies to respond, but Malcolm has wedged himself between his wife and this man.

"Look—I don't know who the hell you are," Malcolm says, his face twisted into a snarl, "but I don't appreciate your stepping to my wife like this."

Cheyenne steps forward and pulls on Malcolm's coat as she momentarily loses sight of Taj. "Honey. Don't!"

Taj, on the other hand, remains still with eyes forward, his gaze boring into Malcolm's forehead. Nicole reaches for Taj's elbow again, connects with it, and tugs him backwards. Taj continues to smile.

"Are you well?" he mouths. Cheyenne nods and sobs harder.

"Taj? Taj?" Nicole yells, pulling harder on his sleeve. "What is going on?"

Malcolm shrugs off Cheyenne's attempt to control him. He steps forward, this time inches from Taj's face. Beads of sweat have appeared on his forehead and baldhead. He wipes at his head forlornly.

"Listen, asshole. Who the fuck are you, and why are you calling my wife Jazz?"

Taj breaks his stare with Cheyenne and locks onto Malcolm. He remains silent.

"I'm talking to *you*, asshole!" Malcolm's finger juts twice into Taj's chest.

Nicole's voice is behind them, rising in pitch and intensity. "Taj, what's going on? Taj, tell me what's going on!"

Taj looks down slowly at Malcolm's fingers,

then back up. He considers his surroundings and steals a glance at Cheyenne, who is pulling on her husband with one hand while wiping her eyes with the other. Mascara is smearing along her full cheekbones. Taj feels a sudden twinge of sadness and turns to leave.

"Where do you think you're going?" Malcolm says loud enough that some of the carolers cease their singing and begin to crowd the space, wondering what the commotion is all about. Seeing that Taj is not paying him any respect or attention, Malcolm grabs for his elbow. Nicole has gripped the back of Taj's coat with her hand.

Taj spins around so suddenly and with such intensity that Nicole has no choice but to loosen her grip on his coat. Again, he bores into Malcolm with those hazel eyes and leans into him until mere inches separate their faces. Taj opens his mouth and whispers to Malcolm: "Don't ever touch me again," he hisses. "You have no idea who you are dealing with. You need to be fearful and walk away."

Cheyenne has attached herself to her husband, pulling and begging him to back off. Nicole is yanking on Taj and becoming frantic. Both men refuse to budge, but Malcolm blinks first.

"Be fearful," Taj repeats, lowering his voice a notch further. "Walk away." Taj breaks his stare with Malcolm, rotating his head slightly so that he can see Cheyenne.

Their eyes meet—briefly.

They lock—then disengage.

And then, Taj turns and leads Nicole through the crowd.

Malcolm remains where he is, nostrils flaring, chest pounding, recalling the intensity of his adversary that has suddenly chilled him to the bone, wondering as he collects his wife and stares her down, *who* was that man?

Two

The thing Taj recalled first—when he dug deep into the recesses of his mind—was the heat. He remembered the terminal, Norman Manley International, a place so small and backwater that he knew for sure he was in a foreign country. Well, yeah, what did he expect?

Here he was, in Kingston, Jamaica, just landed after flying nearly two thousand miles—a journey that took him from the Eastern Shore of Virginia north to New York. He and his pop had looked in the encyclopedia he had borrowed from school to get a sense of where he was going—and where he was going was south, not north. So why then, did he have to travel by air from Norfolk, north to New York's Kennedy, only then to head south? It never made any sense to him.

While deplaning in Kingston the heat had hit

him fast; as he walked down the metal stairs from the jet's belly to the tarmac, the heat had smacked him dead in the face so hard that it took his breath away. This wasn't a little bit of heat—this stuff was downright oppressive!

The second thing that Taj recalled, which had always stuck in his mind, was the soldiers with their weapons—large, black automatic rifles and semi-automatic handguns—big, bulky things that would scare the shit out of any sixteen-year-old—especially one who hadn't been raised on guns.

He was from the Eastern Shore of Virginia, a narrow tract of land between the Chesapeake Bay and the Atlantic Ocean. His father was a waterman. His father's father had been one too. They didn't play with guns or associate with them. Didn't have the inkling to. Handling fish was what Taj's family did—day in and day out.

In the shade of the terminal lobby, a corrugated aluminum building with Coca-Cola signs displayed every hundred feet or so (the branded red and white logo that is internationally recognized), Taj waited among the hordes of Jamaicans—black people with downtrodden eyes. Taj had seen blacks before—his father and relatives are dark-skinned as well—but here there was a sea of them. A few stared back at him, a few nodded silently, their long dreads swaying as they moved, but most ignored him. Which was okay with him.

Taj's very first plane ride had gone fairly well. He had been scared—had talked to his pop about *it—asked him the night before he was to leave whether there was anything to worry about. And Pop had looked him in the eye and said no, there was nothing to fear. Taj nodded, considered his pop's response for a time, and then asked if he had ever taken a plane. Pop regarded him silently for a moment before shaking his head.*

They had encountered some turbulence just past Miami, up around 37,000 feet. The plane had been buffeted around a bit, not very much, but enough to scare Taj into thinking he was going to die—until the woman sitting two seats away (a quiet white woman with glassy blue eyes) reached over and patted his tense knuckles, told him that what they were feeling was normal, and that everything was going to be alright.

He felt like kissing the ground when they finally touched down in Kingston, but as he headed for the tarmac the heat had slapped him silly. Then he suddenly was aware of the guns and soldiers. Well, he momentarily forgot all about turbulence and that kind of nonsense.

Taj was part of a church mission, a small group of folks who were heading to the mountains of Jamaica to help build a community. He had been selected from hundreds of teenagers in his congregation. Why, he never really knew—but he was honored to be going. His guidance counselor at the high school had told him that this was indeed a once-in-a-lifetime opportunity to see how other people in a different part of the world lived. Okay, he wasn't traveling half way around the world, but Taj got the point.

A very small group was to go on this trip and remain for a month. Taj had very much wanted his pop to go with him, but that just wasn't going to happen. Pop couldn't afford to be off from work for one single day, least of all thirty. Besides, in New York they would be joined by four other individuals—two other high schoolers, like himself, and their guardians from their respective churches. In addition, there were supposed to be a dozen or so folks already there in the mountains. Taj and these new people were cycling in; others would be cycling out over the course of the upcoming month.

Sitting in the terminal, wiping the perspiration from his forehead (wishing like hell he had had the forethought to corn roll his afro), his knapsack and oversized suitcase beside him, Taj glanced around, trying to ascertain which folks were in his group and making the final leg of the journey with him.

And then he saw her—coming around a corner, a shiny blue Samsonite trailing behind her, bell-bottom jeans, sandals, and a flowery patterned shirt that accentuated her burgeoning breasts. She was about five seven, with a thin waist, a golden bronze complexion, and thick frizzy dark hair that hung halfway down her back. He put her at no more than seventeen—Taj had never seen anyone so beautiful in all of his short life. He sat there, enthralled, watching her, unable to move, his limbs glued to his sides, feeling the adrenaline surge through him. His mouth dried up, even though he had no intention of speaking.

She walked with an older woman who Taj guessed was her mother (who was shorter, a bit plump, and wore her hair in a much more conservative, shorter style) but had the same face—half Indian, half something else—probably black. The girl was beautiful like he had never seen before, with high cheekbones, a thin nose, and sculpted features—a hint of American Indian, but with a skin tone that told Taj she was mixed.

Taj spent the next forty-five minutes watching her every move—the sketchbook that he had brought with him laid in his lap, untouched. (Taj knew that he wanted to be an architect, so he carried a sketchbook with him wherever he went, capturing ideas on the white pages.)

By the time they announced his flight (he overheard some Jamaicans call it a puddle jumper) he had completed three separate fantasies with this stunningly beautiful girl as his co-star. Of course, Taj never spoke to her—he couldn't actually go to her and just say something. Taj wasn't confident around girls, never had been. He was well liked in school, but never found the right words to say to girls—so he, for the most part, left them alone.

And then she was rising along with her mother as they called the flight—his flight—and Taj felt his stomach burn. The same queasy feeling that had come over him at 37,000 feet returned—yet he was on solid ground. He watched her as she gathered *her things and headed for the plane. He followed slowly, his mind and heart racing, mesmerized, like a lamb to the slaughter.*

The tarmac was on fire—or so it seemed. The asphalt appeared to be smoldering. Taj guessed it was just the heat. Beyond the gate was a Beech King Air Turbo-prop. As he trudged toward it, his bags trailing behind him, he watched the girl—the sensual way her hips swayed and the way she ran her hand down the side of her face, pushing her thick hair behind her ear. It would remain that way for a good half-minute or so before falling out of place again— and just that simple act, of raising a bronze arm to her face, was driving Taj crazy. What it was, he couldn't figure. But it made him feel . . . very good . . . .

The plane wasn't large—Taj counted five round portholes on the side of the white fuselage with red and black trim, so he figured it would seat a dozen passengers at the most. He glanced behind him and saw no one else except a Jamaican with long black dreads held down by a yellow bandana, carrying a single black bag, slowly limping toward him. A thick black walking cane was used for support, and Taj noticed that the handle was intricately carved; the bottom, however, was as smooth as a blade of grass. The man wore an expressionless face behind black sunglasses. The pilot, Taj guessed, was already on board.

At the doorway, a dark woman with bright teeth smiled and, in a thick accent, directed everyone to leave their bags by the rear of the plane. A well-muscled Jamaican was stowing those in the cargo hold.

Taj reached the tiny steps that were built into the fuselage. He climbed slowly, conscious of his head—he was already over six feet tall. The stewardess smiled and motioned for him to take a seat. Taj glanced around the tight cabin, saw that the girl and her mom had taken one set of cracked leather seats two rows up from the door. She was reaching for something in her knapsack when he entered—and glanced up momentarily. Taj stopped, sucked in a breath, as her gaze roamed over him, stopping at his eyes. He decided to smile after some slight deliberation and gave her a weak one, but the girl neither returned it nor held his gaze for a moment longer. She went back to what she was doing—rummaging through her knapsack, as if he weren't even there.

Deflated, Taj took a seat at the back of the plane and next to the window, pushing away thoughts of this girl, replacing them instead with thoughts of his pop.

Three

The interior of the limousine is murky, and for that she is grateful. Malcolm wasted no time getting on his cell and calling for his driver. The car arrived shortly thereafter. As they settle into the posh leather seats, he slams the door; the richness and excitement of a New York Christmas is left outside, sucked out like noxious air.

Malcolm directs the driver to take them back to the hotel. He is short and to the point, and Cheyenne winces because she feels for him. There is no need to direct his anger at the driver, and yet he does.

"I cannot, for the life of me, figure out just what the fuck occurred back there," Malcolm says, turning in his seat to glare at his wife. "Just who was that guy, and more importantly, who is he to you?"

Cheyenne is staring out her window. As they turn onto one of thousands of side streets in Manhattan she notices a horse and carriage trotting alongside of them. The couple is snuggled together under a blanket as the snow falls. It is all so romantic and for a moment, she forgets all about what has just transpired—perhaps it was all a bad dream— except that in this case she was elated to see *his* face after all of these years. To know that he is well fills her with delight. But she pushes all thoughts out of her head and instead concentrates on the horse and carriage, until Malcolm's voice booms at her, shattering her peace.

"I'm talking to you!" He says this with a hiss, as if he doesn't want the driver to hear, even though the privacy shield is raised.

"I am not hard of hearing," she snaps in reply.

"Well, if you would do me the courtesy of answering my fucking questions—"

Cheyenne is preparing to cut him off with a quick snap of her head, but thinks twice about it. What she wants to say to Malcolm is: "I am still your wife, in case you have forgotten—do not speak to me in that tone." Instead, she says this matter-of-factly: "Please honey, I really don't like it when you talk like that." She knows her place, but right now her husband is way out of line. (But she's not going to tell him that.) Malcolm glares at Cheyenne.

"I am not going to stand here and be humiliated in the middle of a goddamned—"

"No one is humiliating you!" Cheyenne almost laughs and runs a hand through her hair. "Why do you always have to exaggerate things?"

"And why do you always deflect situations from the main issue? Who the hell is that guy? Answer that!"

"He is nobody." Cheyenne turns away, still reeling from seeing *him* after so many years.

"Bullshit." Malcolm grabs her arm. "He is somebody to you."

Cheyenne pulls away, giving him an irritated look. "It doesn't matter."

"It does to me."

And Cheyenne realizes that once again, this argument, like so many, comes down to control. Things between them are wonderful when Malcolm is in control—and shitty when he isn't. Malcolm likes to run his marriage like his company—with an iron fist. She glances out the window silently, shaking her head.

Malcolm's hot zone has been breached, the threshold crossed. His face is flushed, and even in the semi-darkness of the limo, Cheyenne can see it. "Cheyenne, why the hell was he calling you Jazz?"

Cheyenne pivots in her seat, the leather groaning in agony. "Look—" she says, exasperated. "He's a friend. An old friend, okay? And 'Jazz' is a name he used to call me, that's all. Now drop it, Malcolm!"

"No, Jazz, I won't drop it," he hisses. "No I won't." Malcolm goes into the interior breast pocket of his camelhair coat and extracts a silver case. He flicks it open, takes a cigarette out, and lights it. He exhales forcefully to the ceiling as his cell phone rings. Cheyenne waves the smoke away and moves to another seat.

"This is M.D. Speak!" He commands. Malcolm listens for a moment then laughs. He begins a rapid-fire discussion that Cheyenne tunes out. Reaching for the controls to the stereo, she finds a jazz station and turns up the volume.

Outside the snow continues to fall. She observes the people on the sidewalks, trudging through the snow, bundled up, carrying gifts home for loved ones, breath escaping from blued lips as they converse about joyful things, she imagines, since holidays are supposed to be blissful and pleasurable.

"Bet you fucked him?" Malcolm says into the cell, interrupting the tranquility of her vision, causing the citadel that she has carefully erected to come crashing down—and in an instant Cheyenne realizes he is speaking to her.

* * *

AWAKENING

Nicole's silence is unnerving—and yet completely expected.

Taj and Nicole, her arm entrusted to him as if a sacred jewel, walk together past a small park whose tree limbs are lit up—decorated with thousands of bright holiday lights—lights that wind up and down each branch and trunk like a serpent, lights that strobe to an hushed rhythm. They find a park bench, dust off the freshly fallen snow with gloved hands, and sit for a moment enjoying the peacefulness and silence. Dozens of coupled adults and children walk through the square. A light breeze has taken flight sending the tree limbs into a gentle dance, the lights writing indecipherable calligraphy into the nighttime air.

Nicole stares directly ahead, her expression showing indifference. Yet Taj knows she is deep in thought. Several youngsters are engaged in a snowball fight and one arcs dangerously close to Nicole's head. She smiles as Taj studies the row of buildings across the street.

One thing about Washington, Taj considers as he scans the steel horizon in front of him. It doesn't have that city feel of Manhattan, largely because of the absence of skyscrapers—those soaring creations that strain to reach heaven. And it is these skyscrapers that fascinate Taj. It is the *simplicity* of them that has attracted his attention since he was a young boy—simplicity from a design standpoint—

and yet the multitude of design variations excites him, the way ice cream does children. So many ways to construct a building. So many ways to solve a similar problem.

"Are you going to tell me, Taj?" Nicole's soft voice breaks the silence. Taj exhales slowly, watching his breath materialize in front of him. He remains silent.

"She's someone to you—that much is clear." Nicole's gaze remains fixed in front of her. Then she turns to him and Taj has no choice but to look her way.

"Nikki—it's not important," he says, reaching for her arm.

Nicole ponders this for a moment. Taj watches her silently. He knows her—understands her all too well—she is studying his words, watching his body language—her routine, utterly predictable.

"If I'm asking, then it is."

Taj considers this.

Women are not difficult to comprehend, he reflects, contrary to public opinion, as many men have been led to believe. There will be those who won't agree—but to Taj, those men just haven't been paying attention. Women are creatures of habit. They say and do the same things over and over again. Study women, Taj is fond of saying, study their patterns, behaviors, moods, thought patterns and, in particular, what they say, and you will have mastered the art of women.

Easier said than done.

Taj sighs, not because he is tired—which he is not—but as a man of few words, he doesn't see the point in continuing. But he knows that to say this would not be fruitful.

"Nikki, I would prefer not to talk about it."

"Because there is something to hide."

A statement, not a question.

"No."

"Care to elaborate?"

Taj sighs again. He stands, dusting off the snow from his coat and reaches for her hand, signaling their time to leave. "Nikki, this is a conversation that I do not wish to have. But if you have to know *something*, I will tell you this. The woman I saw was someone I knew a long, long time ago. Honestly, we shared an intimate relationship, but not in the sense that most people think." He starts to continue but throttles down, reversing his mind. He walks onward.

"Intimate relationship," she says, almost whispering, "care to . . ."

Taj whirls around, stopping Nicole in her tracks. "This is a conversation I do not wish to have!"

Nicole retreats, surprised by his anger. She observes him standing there, beautiful in the shadow of the holiday-lit trees, snow falling lightly, the city sky as a picturesque backdrop, and yet she is concerned by this sudden turn of events. It is out of character for Taj. But she doesn't get angry—no, that is not her style. She reaches out for him—a gloved hand that connects with his smooth face, the way Taj did earlier with this stranger, a woman named Jazz.

She smiles as she moves into his space. He remains in place as she comes to him. Her lips brush up against his cheek, and Taj feels her mouth open as it settles against his skin.

He closes his eyes and hears her say: "We're soul mates, Taj—you and I and I . . . I just want to know what's going on . . . make sure you're okay, that's all."

Taj smiles, reaches for her and returns the kiss—mouth-to mouth—stirring as he experiences the suppleness of her warm flesh.

"I'm okay," he says reassuringly, as he wraps his limbs around her, yet, there are thoughts and images already bubbling to the surface that he can't control—images he thought were long ago hidden and inaccessible.

Four

*T*he Beech King Air rolled gently into the afternoon sky with Taj's nose pressed to the window. The tarmac fell away as the plane's wings dipped, and Taj could see Kingston Harbour spread out before him, its clear blue-green waters inviting. Their destination was a short ride away—about half an hour, no more—a dirt landing strip on a stretch of hills in the Blue Mountains, north from Spanish Town. From there, a jeep would take them to their destination, where the church mission was constructing housing for the poor.

Taj swept his gaze around the interior of the plane. It was small and not at all filled as he had expected; besides himself, the girl and her mother, and the Jamaican who had taken one of the two seats facing rearward behind the cockpit, the plane was empty. Taj has said nothing to any of the passengers. They said nothing to him.

The plane climbed, its engines whining. Taj, fascinated, kept his nose pressed to the glass, observing the countryside roll below them. It amazed him how small things appeared when airborne—people became worker ants trudging along dusty roadways, cars and buses developed into bug-like creatures that seemed to slide along the crooked streets and boulevards. Buildings, even tall ones, lost their perspective from this height, and ultimately became difficult to discern.

Taj could see the pilot up front in the left seat: a dark-skinned, middleaged man, the back of his white shirt damp from sweat, his pilot's cap stuck on his head at an upturned angle. He swept his gaze back to the Jamaican whose stare remained fixed in front of him. The sunglasses stayed on, the black cane clutched tightly in one hand. Taj strained his neck over the top of the leather seat in front of him to see the girl. She was talking with her mother who was in the window seat.

The Jamaican reached down, rummaged in his bag, and removed a silver flask. He removed the top and took a long swig, tipping his bandana-covered head back to the bulkhead. He finished up, wiped his mouth with the back of his hand, and screwed the top back in. He smiled and removed his sunglasses.

"Me name's Seifu," he said, his deep voice rising above the drone of the engines. He seemed to be staring at Taj when he spoke this. "Means 'sword' in

Swahili." He turned to stare at the girl and her mother, and smiled briefly before continuing. "Me frum Africa, da muthaland, but ain't we all? Ain't we all?"

Taj heard the mother mumble something, but was not able to understand her.

"Wat be yur name, pretty sista?" he asked the girl a few rows away. Taj witnessed her shift uncomfortably in her seat.

"Cheyenne," she answered softly.

"Ah. Cheyenne. And dat be yur mum besides yu?"

"Yes."

Seifu snapped his glance to Taj. "And yu strong brudder back der wid da wild eyes—wat dey call yu?"

Taj was momentarily taken aback. He was used to folks staring at his eyes, the dichotomy between darkness and light, but this felt entirely different. He swallowed the fear that seemed to rise up like bile in his throat and responded.

"I am Taj," he said, his voice clear. Cheyenne glanced back and stared for a moment.

"So—we got Cheyenne and her mum der. We got Taj over der. Wat kinda name be Taj, yung brudder? Tell us," he commanded, stretching his arms wide. The cane remained in his fist. Taj didn't like this man called Seifu or the cane—didn't like him one bit.

"My pop . . ." he said, "My father named me Taj after the Taj Mahal in India," Taj responded, thinking about Pop and how he already missed

35

him. Taj had, in the past six hours, traveled farther than his father or his father's father ever had. That thought weighed heavily on him.

The Jamaican began to laugh, throwing his head back, striking the bulkhead in the process. The plane leveled off, the engines throttled back, and Taj noticed lush green jungles had replaced the dirty urban sprawl. The canopy of trees glided beneath them like an unworn blanket that heaved with the swell of hillsides.

"Ah yeah, de Taj Mahal, frum India! Yu not look like no Indian brudders me dun seen!" Seifu laughed again.

That was true, but Taj was silent.

"Cat got yur tung, yung brudder?" Seifu pronounced, raising the flask again to dark lips. He took a swig, his eyes never leaving Taj. "Ah, dat be sum good brew!" He held the flask out at arm's length. "Want sum a dis, brudder Taj?"

Taj shook his head and said, "No thank you."

"Dis here put hair on da chest, dat fer shur!" He cackled again, and the flask shook as he laughed. Cheyenne turned in her seat and glanced at her mother, searching for answers. Seifu rose from his seat, leaning on the black cane for support. He reached out for the first row of seats and moved forward, holding the flask out. "Yu shur, yung brudder?" Not waiting for a response he swung it to Cheyenne. "Bout yu, pretty sista? Jus take wun sip der and yu're hooked fer life!"

Cheyenne withdrew into the leather folds of her seat. Her mother was silent. Seifu shrugged to himself, tipped the flask up, and drank its contents. He then spun around, a move that surprised all of them, and made it back to his seat. He remained poised there for a moment, seemingly deep in thought, contemplating something, before he moved to the left and forward toward the cockpit.

"Les see if dem pilots wanna taste de brew," Taj heard him say. Seifu leaned down, clearing the doorway. The pilot turned slightly, sensing a person in the cockpit with him. Taj could hear them speaking. It was soft and indiscernible over the whine of the engines, and he couldn't help but feel a rising sense of panic that stretched out like the lush canopy below. Taj willed himself to breathe and focus on the scenery outside the glass. He glanced at his watch— they'd been in the air for less than ten minutes— soon now they would begin their descent. Not long now before they'd be back on solid land. His chest thumped, counting away the seconds with its cadence.

The rise of voices from the cockpit caused Taj's gaze to snap forward. And as he struggled to decipher what was being said, he heard Seifu's voice, deep and rising above the engine's drone, saying something loud and undistinguishable before the pilot uttered his sharp rebuttal.

"Back to your seat!"

A flash as Seifu's arm came up, his denim jacket

billowing as Taj strained to see, the seatbelt tightening around his waist, the fear keeping him frozen in place.

The plane lurched, down and to the right, a sudden and terrorizing movement that caused Cheyenne to scream out.

Her mother yelled, "Sweet Jesus, oh my God!"

On the floor of the aisle, the black cane rolled, snapping loudly against metal.

Taj opened his mouth to scream—yet nothing emerged.

His light eyes bulged with the realization they were falling to earth . . . the plane careening out of control, the dense emerald mountainside rushing to meet them, way too fast . . .

Five

Apple martinis make everything important seem trivial—at least it appears that way to Cheyenne. They are at The Hype, the newest trend-setting club in Manhattan, a stone's throw from the Village, for a CD release party—not someone on Malcolm's label. But in this business, image is as much a part of the music scene as being musically creative. And nowadays, more so.

So, here she sits, with an entourage of people she hardly knows, on curved, low leather couches so soft she keeps stroking the hide in a sensuous way—quite unconsciously, for there is nothing about this crowd that turns her on. She is thinking about *him.*

Taj.

Those eyes that light up the night.

Eyes that speak to her with their intensity and passion.

Stop it.

Cheyenne reaches for her apple martini, marvels at the emerald green liquid as she takes a sip; it is potency that soothes, yet strikes simultaneously. And that's when she realizes that everything in this world turns insignificant after a few martinis.

Malcolm obviously agrees. The fire that had been stoked in the limo has simmered down, and is on the verge of being blown *out*. He sits not far from her; a half-dozen video models surrounding him like moths to a flame—deep in conversation—about his next project, the music biz, this and that. Cheyenne isn't interested in what Malcolm has to say or in the beautiful young women who hang on every word he articulates. She is attempting to concentrate—focus her brain like a laser, open the annals of her mind and search deep within its recesses for that which she had cleverly hidden away, packed tight, like knickknacks from previous generations that have been sequestered away in the back of a dusty hot attic.

Malcolm is smiling. And why shouldn't he? To his left is a Latino model who has appeared in several of his label's music videos. To his right, a chocolate goddess whose name escapes Cheyenne, but she is a B-movie actress who allegedly began her career in porn. And why wouldn't she, Cheyenne muses, with tits like that.

The actress catches Cheyenne's eye and smiles. Cheyenne returns the grin as if the two of them are close girlfriends. Malcolm glances in her direction and quickly turns his gaze away. Cheyenne smiles to no one in particular as the hip-hop music blares from overhead speakers.

Simmering down, on the verge of being blown out . . . Malcolm has not mentioned the church incident to her since they arrived thirty minutes ago. But he will. He's just waiting for the opportune time.

Cheyenne gets up, excuses herself from the crowd, and walks away. The room is smoke-filled, loud, and crammed with pretentious people. She walks to the bar, passing well-dressed men and women who cease conversations as she glides by. Cheyenne is wearing a tight short black sequined dress with a diamond broach necklace and matching earrings—simple yet elegant. Her hair is worn down and long. She is, in a word, stunning.

Reaching one of The Hype's many bars, she gets the attention of the bartender and orders another martini. Sipping it slowly, she ponders the seeing of Taj again after all of these years. How long has it been? Twenty years?

My God.

The tears begin to flow, surprising her with their emergence, like an avalanche. A hand on her shoulder forces her to look up and around. Malcolm.

"Why are you crying?"

"Why do you care?"

"You're still my wife."

"Funny. You weren't treating me like one earlier."

Malcolm pauses at this. Cheyenne uses the opportunity to dab at her eyelashes and cheeks. Malcolm reaches for her arm.

"I want to leave," he says. "Head back home. In the morning."

Cheyenne has a look of incredulity on her face. "Why?" she asks, her mind racing, searching his features for a clue. "I thought we were staying another week?"

Malcolm's face shifts—morphs into a seething grin. He hisses when he speaks next.

"I'll tell you why—because I am no longer *feeling* New York."

"What are you talking about?" she says softly in a womanly, unquestioning tone.

"Don't feel like running into any more of your friends, you feel me?"

The sneer that Malcolm has painted on his face is so phony that Cheyenne feels like screaming. There are so many thoughts swirling around in her head, but she doesn't have the time or inkling to sort them out.

Instead, she rises off the barstool and heads silently for the door.

Malcolm lets her go without blinking.

Midnight. The snow has ceased. A whitish glow bathes their hotel suite. The lights are extinguished; the vertical blinds are opened. Cheyenne lies prone on the oversized bed, her black sequined dress hitched around her thighs.

She is alone, heading back home in the morning.

No. She can't leave. Not yet. Not before she sees *him* once again.

But how? There are more than eight million people in New York City—probably a million more tourists this week alone. Is he a resident here? Does he live right across town, or is he visiting from out of town like she is?

Cheyenne's legs are opened. Her hand snakes down to massage her inner thigh, feeling the raised spot of puckered flesh. Cheyenne rubs it slowly, using the tips of her fingers to feel the spoiled tissue, the area softening with age, not as rigid and unsightly as it once was. Cheyenne rolls over, as if the act will re-sculpt what was once smooth and innocent.

Standing, she observes herself in the full-length mirror. Her face and form are decorated in shadows. She lifts her dress to look at the spot. The tattoo covers it well—a lavender flower, its petals alluring and inviting.

It's been twenty years.

She hasn't thought about him and their *situation* in so long. And now her head hurts from all of the thoughts. Stop it, she commands herself. This is silly, she tells herself.

And she is sure that the last thing he's doing right now is thinking about her. Right? She is a married woman, in love with her husband—his faults, temper, and all. Besides, she's sure that he has found someone. Cheyenne wasn't so rocked with astonishment when he uttered those words that she didn't notice the striking woman standing behind him.

Taj.

My God.

Staring at herself in the mirror—Cheyenne suddenly makes up her mind. She's going out. Tonight.

To find him . . . if she can.

The limo takes the corner slowly as Cheyenne lounges in the back. Soft jazz emanates from speakers. The music soothes her, calming her nerves.

She thinks about what she's doing, trying to find a needle in a haystack, and shakes her head knowingly. It's crazy—the chances minute of spotting him in this city hours after she first heard those words again, after so many years. But if she doesn't try, she won't forgive herself.

The driver is steering the vehicle down Eighth Avenue. Cheyenne is scanning the sidewalks, her mind and eyes alert.

Back at the hotel she Googled him from her phone. Nothing.

And so, she roams the streets as the next best thing, hoping, praying he will be found. Spotted on a corner, upturned collar, those calming eyes searching for *her* . . .

Up Broadway, around the theater district, past now-closed shops and restaurants, folks still milling about, but none, no one resembling him.

No sign of Taj.

Cheyenne directs the driver back to the church. They arrive fifteen minutes later.

The street is desolate and calm. It is almost two a.m. She is not thinking of Malcolm, the party, or what she will say to him when she returns.

The limo sits in front of the darkened church. Cheyenne remains inside the warm vehicle, the soft jazz calming her nerves. She has no reason to be jumpy, but she can't control what she is feeling.

Seconds turn to minutes. Minutes grow into

tens of minutes. A half hour later, Cheyenne heads back to the hotel and the comfort of a warm bed.

Malcolm is waiting for her when she returns.

"Where have you been?" He doesn't raise his voice, yell, or grab at her arm. But she is scared nonetheless.

"Out," she says, swallowing hard.

"Couldn't sleep?" Malcolm asks, through a martini-infused haze.

Cheyenne remains silent as she gets undressed. He watches her move from the bedroom to the bathroom and shut the door, hears her run the water, and then sees her return a while later. The lights remain off, but the interior is bright from the snow. Shadows from the street paint the walls with eerie designs.

Cheyenne gets into bed, reaches for Malcolm who is on his back, staring at the ceiling. She kisses his cheek and lies down.

"Bet you fucked him . . ." Malcolm whispers before turning on his side, giving his back to his lovely wife.

Cheyenne sighs inaudibly, knowing sleep will be hard to come by.

The sky has yet to lighten when she feels him. It is a slow, indiscernible sensation that doesn't register at first due to her slumber, but then she recognizes it. Malcolm has turned to face her and closed the distance between their sleeping forms until nothing separates them. His body is flush with hers, spooning Cheyenne as he wraps an arm across her sleeping torso and pulls her gently to him. Beneath the blankets he is becoming firm. He presses himself lightly into her backside, a proposition that might have gone unnoticed if he hadn't repeated it. But he did. Cheyenne is breathing regularly when her eyes flutter and she wakes up, settling back into her husband with a sigh, thankful for his warmth and comfort. She senses him move again, a slight repositioning veiled in the act of retightening his arms around her as a harried breath escapes from his lips; a slow deep pelvic thrust signals his intentions. He has positioned himself strategically, his now fully hard organ fitting snuggly into the valley of her back. Her tee shirt has ridden up, helped by his hand, which has dipped below the covers and the fabric of her top as he searches for her stomach. His fingertips glide across firm skin, feeling the contoured well of her navel before moving toward the rise of her breasts. Cheyenne cannot help but press against him as he catches a thick strand of hair between his lips while nuzzling against her neck, cupping her breast in his hand. Malcolm brushes her hair back from the neck, baring her skin. She looks beautiful lying there, her bronze skin and dark curls distinctive in the contrasting whiteness of the hotel room. The snow has resumed falling; large snowflakes that catch the light from soaring glass and steel structures gently drift to the ground as he kisses the cord in her neck. Malcolm rises up on his elbow, his fingertips tracing her outline beneath the comforter.

Cheyenne is wondering what he is thinking . . .

He bends to kiss her, lightly tasting her lips before his hands disappear beneath the covers, searching for her soft spots. Her legs part as he strokes her thigh, allowing his fingers to dance above the silk lace of her panties. Malcolm bends forward as he thrusts the covers aside, raising her tee shirt as he marvels at her lovely body. Cheyenne shivers uncontrollably as her nipples are bared—they tighten and stretch as his hand covers them quickly.

"Cold in here," she whispers, draping a forearm around his neck.

"I can fix that," he muses. Rising, he crosses the floor to the window to glimpse a peek at the snowfall. Turning, he traverses the room and taps the thermostat on. The whirl from the furnace begins before he has returned to her. She shivers again as he covers her with his body and commences a gentle grind between her exposed thighs as he fondles her neck with his lips. Moving downward, he reaches her clavicle, allowing his tongue to touch and then alight from the bones as if he were playing a game. He cups her breast in one hand, kneads the flesh, softly as first, but then with increased pressure as Cheyenne begins to moan. He plays with her nipple using the flesh of his thumb, rubbing it in circles—in one direction, then the other, as she arches her back, thrusting herself into his waiting mouth. He wets her skin, twirls his tongue around her areola as if bathing her, then shifts to the other, grasping soft tissue and pinching it between his fingers, attacking her nipple with his tongue and teeth, grazing over skin and nibbling ever so slightly—the way Cheyenne likes.

His hand snakes down her writhing stomach to her panty line, slipping underneath, quietly and stealthily before reaching her mound that is moist to the touch. Cheyenne parts her legs further, allowing her husband to invade her crevice with his fingers. Her eyes are blazing, the heat surrounding her consoling as her fingers trace a meandering path through his chest hair down to his stomach. Descending further, she touches the bulb of his solid penis that stretches toward his waist; she rubs her palm against it before encircling the girth between her fingers. Lightly squeezing, feeling his pulse and his readiness—sensing her own desire, she is no longer concerned about what he is thinking, no longer wondering if Malcolm remains fixated on *him*. Thankful that for the moment his mind is elsewhere . . .

She is grateful for the rejuvenating warmth that spreads outward from her core toward her limbs. Cheyenne can feel her fingertips tingle and her toes quiver as Malcolm slips her panties down until she takes over and flings them away from her ankle. They vanish as they become lodged in the folds of the comforter that lies heaped at the foot of the bed.

He enters her with a slow graceful motion. Silently they glide against each other, Malcolm controlling the tempo as he nuzzles his head between her shoulder and neck. He employs full strokes that begin with his head breaching her budding lips, suspended in space for a moment, poised at the narrow opening that is sodden with juices, before plunging deep within, bearing down until his entire shaft is shrouded by her irresistible vessel.

And then intermission—a pause when Malcolm rests atop of Cheyenne, settling in, "soaking" as he is fond of saying, allowing them to experience each other during the stillness, feeling her constrict around him as he throbs inside of her before starting up again, reaching for the fleshy part of her thighs as he increases his tempo. Cheyenne moans with pleasure as he fills then drains her repeatedly.

Suddenly she senses a change in his cadence. He is grasping her thighs with a bit more pressure than usual, bearing down, moving in and out of her with an increased, frenzied rhythm, like ocean waves whipped into a frothy mix by a brewing storm, his fingers digging into her skin until the flesh reddens. She tells him to stop, but he is unrelenting and seemingly hard of hearing.

Malcolm is out of control.

Cheyenne cries out as he buries his face in the pillow, stretching her legs upward as he forces her thighs further apart. He is pummeling her now, his body an engine, a machine running on automatic—he neither sees her wince nor responds when she attempts to push him away. Finally, after pounding his back and sides with her fists, she manages to get his attention by yanking a fistful of chest hair. Malcolm swats her hand away as he moves off her sweating body.

"What is *wrong* with you?" she shrieks. Cheyenne rolls away from her husband and onto her stomach, as her hands rush to her thighs, massaging the spots that burn where Malcolm has hurt her.

"I can't believe you're doing this *again.*"

He eyes her silently, his stare flicking down to her healthy flanks and crescent shaped ass, which juts out in an enticing way and appears to glisten in the twilight of the snowfall.

Cheyenne silently contemplates his actions. She stares in disbelief, trying to understand the physical pleasure that he experiences at her expense. But there's something else—a fleeting image emerges—one so haunting that she forces herself back to reality.

Malcolm is on her in an instant, sliding his still erect manhood inside of her from behind as she whips her head around in horror.

"Malcolm!" she yells, "Stop it. You're *hurting* me!"

"Fuck, you feel good!" he groans, forcing his weight down onto Cheyenne, and she is no match for him. He seizes her lower back with both hands, his thumbs along the ridge of her spine as he contains her in his grasp, pressing down as he fucks her, feeling the premonition of orgasm build deep inside of him.

"Stop it, stop it, STOP IT!" Cheyenne pants, unable to scream because of the intensity of his assault.

"Jesus!" Malcolm groans, "Baby, I'm gonna come . . ." he says, gripping her so tightly his fingernails break skin. She feels him come inside her, a stream of warmth that washes into her, a fire without consolation. His movements cease and he crumples on top of her, like a toggle switch that has shut down the fury. Cheyenne shifts away from him as if he were a leper and huddles in the corner of the large bed, knees to her chest as she shivers uncontrollably, her teeth chattering. It takes Malcolm a few minutes to emerge from his post-orgasmic fog to even notice her. He reaches over to stroke her hair but she flinches away.

"Goddamn baby, that was good!" he mutters.

Cheyenne doesn't hear him. She is lost in her own world—hunched over, in a fetal position, shivering, breathing rapidly, and *remembering*...

Malcolm reaches for her again, inquires what is wrong but gets no response.

Remembering...

Shrugging, he kisses the top of her head as he places the comforter over her cowering form. He heads for the shower to wash away the remnants of their lovemaking, leaving her to flounder in her anguish, alone.

Six

Northeast D.C. The air at two a.m. is clear and still—no breeze to gently nudge tree limbs into a dance recital. No birds are singing; they have long since left for a warmer province. The street of three-story row houses is quiet— occasionally a car can be heard up the road, the sound of exhaust and low growl as the driver shifts gears, but not here.

The street is lined with cars—each one silent and cold, encased in a thin cocoon of ice. Light from streetlamps reflects off each crystal and is refracted and bounced around, creating a kaleidoscope of dazzling patterns. If one were to awake at this hour and peer out from the window, one would marvel at the winter wonderland, where diamonds encrust everything in sight—leaves, branches, cars, stone steps, lampposts, and mailboxes.

AWAKENING

His bedroom occupies two-thirds of the top floor of a brick row house. The room is medium sized, decorated in simplistic yet modern motif—low cherry wood bed, curved headboard, two squat end tables on either side (perfectly equidistant from each other), crimson red paint adorning the walls, a lone Sawada print above the bed.

Nice.

The bed is occupied with the prone figures of Taj and Nicole. Nicole is fast asleep, on her back, the rise and fall of her breasts following a gentle rhythm. Taj is curled on his side, legs and feet pressed together, wrists and elbows joined, as if bound. Clad in a wife beater and cotton drawstring pants, a layer of sheen covers his body.

Despite the winter cold, Taj is sweating. The tremor begins in his wrists and spreads slowly and methodically through his body. Taj is moaning, softly, almost imperceptibly, little sounds that escape his mouth in a manner that is chaotic and impure. By the time the shudder finally rocks him awake, his face is tense and soaked.

It is the simultaneous scream rising in pitch that awakens Nicole with a start. She rolls over and caresses his damp face, her own face twisting in pain.

"Baby, are you okay?" she asks, gingerly.

A pause to catch his breath. "Yes."

"Third time this week. Baby, what's wrong?"

Taj is silent. He wipes at his forehead with his tee shirt, swings his legs out of bed, and heads for the kitchen on the first floor. He takes the stairs two at a time, forcing himself to concentrate on movement and not what was in his dreams. He returns shortly with a tall glass of water. He stands in front of his windows, consumes the water with a half-dozen gulps, glances out at the quiet street, notes the diamonds and pearls blanketing the street.

On any other night he would find the scene peaceful and serene. He would beg Nicole to come witness the splendor with him, the two of them marveling at the beautiful setting before them.

But not tonight. Instead, he turns to read the clock radio.

Nicole has propped herself up in bed and is watching him silently. The covers are pulled up to her neck—it is cold in the room and she wants no part of this chilly air.

"Come to bed."

"In a minute."

"Taj," Nicole pleads, "talk to me. This thing with the nightmares began on the train home from New York City."

Taj won't fly. He recalls awakening with a jolt somewhere between Newark and Wilmington, his fellow passengers glancing up sharply from their iPads and newspapers as he cried out, as if in pain.

He *was* in pain. And it's only getting worse, but he won't tell Nicole that.

"Listen, baby, you need to talk to me," Nicole begins. "I love you. If we're going to be married I need to know your troubles—regardless of how insignificant they may seem to you."

Taj slips within the warm folds of the comforter after setting down the empty glass. "I'm okay, Nikki, go to sleep."

"No, Taj—we need to talk about this." She turns to him. "Please?"

"There's nothing to talk about." Taj lays his head down and reaches behind him to fluff the pillow. He shoots Nicole a quick glance and smiles as if to say everything is cool, baby. Don't worry.

Nicole leans in, strokes his shoulder with her fingernail.

"But there is, baby," she says softly, her voice cracking. "What is going on, Taj? You aren't communicating like you used to. You're holding everything in and not sharing. That's not healthy." Nicole shakes her head solemnly as she lowers her voice a notch. "I thought we were soul mates, Taj—soul mates are supposed to share everything, remember?"

And Taj sighs—because this conversation, he knows, is long overdue. He sits up, his damp back pressed against the curved cherry wood headboard and looks down at Nicole.

"Okay—let's talk," he says.

"Tell me what's going on, Taj?"

A pause. "I can't."

"Why Taj?" A pleading in her voice as she gazed up at him.

"Because . . ." he reaches out to stroke her face softly. "Because I just can't."

"Because you can't or you won't?"

"It's not that simple."

"And why not? We're two intelligent people—why can't you tell me what's going on? Something surely is."

"Nikki—look, I love you and you have nothing to worry about. I'm just going through something that I need to sort through by myself—alone. Please don't worry."

"How can you say that? Ever since you saw that . . . woman, things have been different between us." Nicole pushes herself up and leans on the headboard to be eye level with Taj. "Don't give me that look, Taj—you know exactly what I'm talking about. Since that night nothing has been the same. You don't talk to me, you're having these crazy nightmares . . ."

"They're not nightmares."

"Bullshit! I wasn't born yesterday, Taj. I know a fucking nightmare when I see it." She takes in a breath.

"Okay, Nicole—"

"No, not okay, Taj. Not okay—I want you to let me in," she pleads, reaching for his arm. "I want to understand why my baby is hurting like this. Remember when you asked me to marry you?"

Taj nods somberly.

"You stared into my eyes and told me about soul mates. You told me how most people spend their entire lives looking for someone who can make them whole—that someone with whom they can share their deepest, darkest secrets. Remember what you said to me that night, Taj? Remember?"

"Yes."

"You said, 'Thank God I've found my soul mate. Thank God I've found you.'"

Taj exhales forcefully. Slowly. He's not angry. He's remembering.

"Nikki—I need to tell you something." He pauses, seeing that he has her full attention. "I remember what I said, and I meant what I said then, and I feel it now."

"Okay."

"But . . ." he takes a breath and forges onward. "Being soul mates does not mean sharing every single feeling, emotion, or thought pattern. It means communicating those things that *need* to be shared—some things shouldn't be shared."

"What?"

"Let me explain, Nikki—you and I are soul mates. I share the vast majority of things with you."

"Vast majority?" Nicole asks, skepticism creeping into her voice.

"In fact, up till now, I have shared everything with you—"

"Exactly," she says, turning to face him squarely. "And that's why this situation is so difficult for me. Because you are shutting me out."

"Not shutting you out, baby. It's just that I'm not ready to let you in yet. I'm not sure if I'm ready to let myself in yet."

"Taj, I'm not sure what all that means. I do know this—one of the reasons I fell in love with you is because of your honesty. You are the most honest man I've ever met—you wear your emotions on your sleeve, and I like that. You tell me what you're feeling: when you're happy, when you're sad. You've told me things that you're not proud of, and I haven't judged you. It's brought us closer, made us stronger as a couple. Please, baby, don't throw all of that away."

Nicole is crying silently, tears scampering down her cheek. She makes no attempt to wipe them away.

"Nikki—please don't cry." Taj reaches for her, places her head against his chest, adjusting the covers over both of them. "It's not like

I'm throwing everything away. This is one instance when . . ." Taj chooses his words carefully, "I need to sort through what I'm feeling on my own *first*. I want to share this with you, honest I do, but I can't do it now, not until it makes sense to me." Taj kisses her forehead. His voice is a near whisper. "Okay?"

Nicole ponders his words. She is staring past him—her eyes fixated on a point in the midst of the window shade. Taj lets her be, not wanting to rush her. He watches her—observes her expression, the lines on her face between cheekbone and mouth—waiting for the sign when the lines will soften. And he will know then that everything is okay. He knows she is weighing his words in her beautiful, sharp, and analytical mind.

That's the main difference between them. Nicole is thinking. Taj is feeling.

He loves her regardless.

Nicole glances at Taj, stares at those hazel eyes that regularly bring stillness and respite to a fanatical world. Abruptly, she turns over on her side and shuts her eyes tight.

Taj looks at her, saying nothing, waiting for her to speak.

She remains silent.

Tonight, she will not be consoled by his mystical eyes.

* * *

Forty-three hours later and Nicole has seen no change in Taj. They've gone on with their lives (a building project that's four months late and two million dollars over budget for him, a string of classes and regular office hours for her), with little contact between them—not at all the norm for Nicole and Taj. Zero discussion regarding Taj's nightmares, and more importantly, the larger issue involving *her*. Nicole decides to take matters into her owns hands and picks up her cell, dials Taj at home, and tells him (instead of asking) that she'll pick him up for a late dinner in Adams Morgan in less than thirty minutes.

Taj knows he has no choice but to be ready.

Nicole arrives within twenty minutes and together they drive up 18th Street to their favorite Ethiopian restaurant. There is little conversation between them; Taj silently scans outside the passenger window of Nicole's sedan while an IndiaArie CD provides the mood. She asks about his day and he responds mechanically, almost without feeling. (This project of his is incredibly hectic and kicking his ass—he'll be damned glad when it's over.) Then silence. She breaks the stillness with chatter about her day and mindless department gossip regarding people whom she's introduced to Taj at faculty functions.

Parking is a bitch in Adams, the collection of diverse restaurants, nightclubs, and bars within a three-block radius that caters to Washington's hippest and chic crowd: white, black, Latino, Asian. The thin track of real estate is always jumping, always crowded regardless of the day or time of the week, an eclectic meeting place for people of color and those who are lacking in pigmentation—from Club Heaven and Hell (Heaven's on the top two floors, Hell's on the bottom), to Felix, Tryst, Montego Bay, Tom Tom, Bukom Café, and Madame Organ's. After circling for nearly ten minutes, Nicole finds a tight spot and backs in her car. When they get out and begin to walk, they find the air crisp and clear. Taj can see his breath fan out as he exhales.

The restaurant is a half-block up on the left. On the way they pass an Italian place, a Mexican café, an Ethiopian restaurant (there are at least four on these two blocks alone), a half-filled club that caters to the college crowd, and a hole-in-the-wall Caribbean joint that is blasting reggae from tiny house speakers. Nicole has looped her arm through Taj's as they walk. He remains silent as if deep in thought.

Up ahead past the Caribbean spot stands a group of black men. They are huddled together in a circle by the curb, smoking cigarettes and talking loudly. A French café with outdoor tables takes up most of the sidewalk. Nicole and Taj squeeze by, Nicole disengaging herself from Taj as he follows, eyeing the men mutely. One man breaks away from the crowd, bumps past Taj, and saunters up to Nicole. He is of medium build, dark skinned, and dreaded. A green, yellow, and black knit cap adorns his head, the colors of Jamaica covering half of his thick locks. Taj watches him touch Nicole's elbow and sees her turn as her eyes narrow and scan his features, recognition absent from her face.

"Can I interest you in some music, pretty lady?" he says with a thick patois drawl. In his hand is a bunch of CDs. Nicole shakes her head as Taj reaches for her arm and elbows the guy forcefully toward the curb.

"Can't you see she's with someone?" Taj asks incredulously.

"No need to shove my brudder," the Jamaican responds, his eyes flicking towards the men who have ceased their conversation. "Besides," he says, moving back to Nicole again, "let me hear it from da fine sista herself dat she's not interested in some reggae and me be moving on den."

Taj had taken Nicole by the arm and moved her swiftly past the café when the Jamaican spoke again. Taj's step falters; Nicole senses it and whispers to him, "Just ignore him, Taj, please."

But he isn't paying attention.

Taj clenches his fists and flexes his arms as

he rams his body into the unsuspecting Jamaican. The guy is thrown off balance and almost falls to the ground. Before he can decipher what is happening, Taj spins around, grabs him by the lapels of his jacket, and thrusts him into the back of a parked SUV. The Jamaican bounces off the spare tire, setting off the car alarm. Taj is on him in an instant as Nicole screams, her shrill hardly rising above the warble of the piercing alarm. Taj pummels the guy's chest with his fists in rapid succession before two Jamaicans yank him off their friend. CDs spill from his hand and pockets, plastic cracking as they hit the pavement; the Jamaican's eyes are bulging and his breath harried as he winces in pain.

"What de fuck's your problem, mon?" he yells, once he sees that Taj has been secured. Taj wriggles like a caged rabid dog. Foam escapes from his lips as he hurls a string of expletives at the Jamaican. Nicole is pleading in vain with him to calm down. The Jamaican brushes himself off and squats down to collect his broken CDs; his entourage eyes Taj with contempt but says and does nothing further. After a few tense moments of men eyeing men quietly, veiled threats transmitted silently among them, the Jamaicans release Taj and move on down the street. He is left alone with Nicole.

"Taj—just what the hell was that about?"

Nicole shouts, tugging at his arm.

Taj's eyes are blazing. Nicole can see he is breathing hard. His fists remained clenched and he nibbles on his bottom lip, his stare never wandering from the Jamaicans who have crossed the street and continue to move away.

"Taj . . . TAJ!" Nicole yells.

His gaze snaps to her after a moment. "What?"

"What? WHAT? You're a madman, that's what. You could have gotten us killed!"

Taj snorts.

"Oh, you're a fighter now—taking on a group of men who could be carrying for all you know."

Nicole shakes her head at his silence.

"You're crazy, you know that?" she quips. She turns, takes four steps before halting, and glares back at him.

"I don't even know who you are anymore," she remarks. Nicole turns on her heel and walks away. Taj stands there, exhaling forcefully, the anger slowly receding below the surface as he watches her go.

"Yeah, you're right—you don't have any idea who I am," he whispers to himself as he turns away from Nicole, his breath still ragged.

No idea at all . . .

Seven

Fear is a shiny tipped sword that repeatedly gouged his flesh until he almost died. Fear is an oversized hand that reached out from behind, covered his mouth, and suffocated him until he almost expired. Fear—plain, unbridled, and raw, almost killed him before Seifu took over.

But it didn't.

Taj relived the horrific pain that shot through his veins as the plane flew out of control, on its side, the lush jungle below a rush of out-of-focus images. He remembered the shouting and screaming—guttural cries whose drone overtook the sound of revving engines.

Cheyenne and her mother were wailing, frantically brandishing their hands over the tops of the seats. Seifu was screaming, too—in a tongue that Taj couldn't decipher—at the near dead or uncon-

scious pilot—Taj couldn't tell. His thought process was shut down. Fear kept him planted in his seat.

Terror and chaos took over.

The plane buffeted and shook. Taj couldn't understand why. What was happening? What had Seifu just done? Who was flying the plane?

Cheyenne's mother attempted to scramble from her seat to the front, but the listing of the plane made that impossible. She clawed at the leather seats, attempting to solicit a hold and move, but was detained against the porthole.

More shouting from the cockpit before the plane righted itself.

Taj threw up, the vomit flying through his splayed fingers onto the seatback in front of him. He was dizzy and beyond terrified—the realization that he was going to die seeped into him, and made him cry.

The tears streamed down his face and he found that he was thinking about his pop—all the things that he would not be permitted to say. As he shivered uncontrollably, he thought: who would help now around the house? Who would Pop talk to when he was dead and gone? Pop would be alone. And that deeply saddened him. This wasn't fair. He never should have agreed to this trip. Never should have left his pop all alone.

The screams had ceased. With the plane righting itself, it was as if everyone hoped and prayed that things were once again well in hand.

That everything would be okay.

Taj, for a moment, believed it, too.

Hope was a reason to live.

Seifu reappeared in the cabin, a wild look in his eyes. He glared at Cheyenne and her mother for a moment before sweeping his stare to Taj. Seifu saw him weeping and emitted a short laugh that was more like a yelp than anything else. He spun around and retreated back into the cockpit.

Cheyenne's mother was up immediately, holding the seats for support. The plane buffeted slightly as she moved toward the front of the cabin. Taj could hear Cheyenne whimpering as her mother gestured for her to move to the back.

Cheyenne, like Taj, was frozen in her seat.

Her mother raised her voice, gestured again.

This time, Cheyenne quickly scurried toward the back.

She was wide-eyed and her face was red, almost splotchy. She wore a look of desperation. Cheyenne made it to Taj's row quickly, and took the seat next to him. He observed her silently, his mouth open, his breath ragged as his gaze flickered from her mother back to her. She was shivering as she fell into the seat. She didn't look at him. Taj wiped his mouth with his sleeve and tried to say something.

Words would not flow.

In the front of the cabin, Cheyenne's mother had reached the cockpit. Taj could hear her arguing with Seifu.

"What are you doing? What in God's name is happening here?"

Seifu was agitated, responding in the indecipherable tongue.

"Mother of Jesus, please don't do this . . ." The rest was cut short as she was shoved out of the cockpit by a force that threw her to the floor. Cheyenne screamed and jumped up, but Taj reached for her and caught her arm. She glared at him before the plane turned sharply and nosed up, forcing her back into her seat.

Taj could hear her mother's whimpers. Cheyenne was yelling for her mother to get up. With tears streaming down her face, she pleaded with her to crawl toward the back. Taj held onto the armrests, his knuckles ashen, and his mouth open in horror as nausea struck his abdomen, causing him to almost faint. His head slammed against the porthole as the plane took another insanely tight turn. Taj felt himself losing control, wondering if this was what dying felt like.

Then they were horizontal again. As quickly as the terror had begun, it ceased; the only sound in the cabin was the steady drone of engines.

Taj glanced out the window. The only frame of reference that made sense was seeing the earth from this window, and knowing they still had a chance.

The thriving rain forest was back with its comforting unbroken green canopy.

Taj felt lightheaded. He was breathing rapidly, knew he was going to vomit again, and was desperately trying to will it away. Cheyenne's head was be-

tween her legs, an outstretched hand reaching for her mother who remained on the floor.

The plane twisted in the air and shook violently once again. More screams of terror . . .

Taj remembers turning his head as the vomit rushed from his mouth, uncontained, and seeing blue sky in the porthole.

Blue sky . . .

Before his eyes closed shut.

His eyes snap open. Taj catapults himself off the couch with such intensity that it injures the muscles in his back and neck. He is covered in sweat and panting. The pain spikes through his shoulders making him wince.

Nicole is staring at him wide-eyed, chanting, "What's wrong? What's wrong?"

Oh my God.

It takes Taj a few seconds to calm himself down. He remains standing, willing his heart muscles to slow down, his light eyes darting from left to right as if they were pin balls, seeing what is not literally in front of him.

Blue sky . . .

Taj opens his mouth, and then quickly shuts it. No words emerge.

He's thinking about blue sky.

He remembers.

He recalls.

Everything.

It is vivid. He is there. He is living it.

Again . . .

Groaning, he nearly collapses to the couch. Nicole is there to catch him and reel him in, wrapping her arms around his quivering frame and pulling him to her bosom. Soothingly she strokes him.

"Baby, are you okay?"

"Yes." It comes out as a croak.

"Nightmare." A statement, not a question. Nicole knows.

"No," Taj says, as her face swims in and out of focus before the clarity sharpens.

"This shit is for real."

Eight

The sound of singing permeates the morning air, mixing with the aroma of frying bacon and freshly brewed coffee. A Les Nubians song is playing in the background. Cheyenne is alone; she backs away from the range where a three-cheese omelet is cooking. Taking the ends of her apron in her hands, she begins to groove to the song, singing along with the duo, but in a different pitch and melody, taking the music to a new level, her rendition of the French lyrics soulful and rhythmic. She bends down, gripping the ends of the apron, jutting her ass out from the confines of her satin shorts, shaking it provocatively as she feels the beat, letting it flow through her, melding with her fluids and bones until she and the song's pulse are one, her body writhing like a disturbed cobra.

Malcolm watches her silently from the expanse of the next room.

They are back in L.A., their palatial single-level home on the edge of a canyon where coyotes can be heard howling at twilight. She is in the kitchen. He observes her from behind a polished steel column in the corner of the sunken living room, a vast area filled with bone leather, teakwood, and vibrant artwork.

She continues to sing, unaware that she is being observed, her long frizzy hair free flowing, and arcing from left to right as she imitates an Egyptian dancer. Malcolm is full with desire as he watches his wife's motion. Carnal thoughts invade his mind as he observes her hips and sculpted ass tremble. But it is more than cravings of passion with him—it is during times like these, when he observes her unfettered, free from her own self-consciousness and anxiety, that she blossoms, like a tulip spreading its nectar-spiced petals—and he knows with conviction that he truly loves his wife.

Malcolm enters the kitchen, sliding his arms around Cheyenne's body. He pulls her to him, reaches down, and finds a soft breast under the folds of her satin top as he kisses her neck. Cheyenne leans into him, closing her eyes, continuing her singing and slow groove—pushing her ass into his pelvis as they connect, the two synchronized to the beat as he kneads her flesh, their fervor intensifying.

"Good morning," she says seductively when the song dies.

"Yes it is." Malcolm turns her around and kisses her squarely on the mouth. Tastes the flavor of bacon on her lips.

"I've made an omelet for you, honey. I hope you are hungry."

"For your cooking—shit, yeah. Bring it on!"

They take breakfast on the stone deck overlooking the canyon. The air is low sixties—Malcolm dons a sweatshirt, Cheyenne a denim jacket—as a light breeze gently caresses them. They talk about Malcolm's schedule, studio work after the holidays, and their trip to New York.

They've been home for three days. Malcolm hasn't mentioned the incident since they returned. But he will.

Cheyenne talks about a new project that she expects to embark on after the holidays. She plans to photograph a little-known Indian tribe in Arizona, spend time observing them in their native surroundings, and capture their habits on film. A freelance piece that she's pitched to National Geographic Channel. Malcolm listens attentively in between bites of his omelet, asking a few questions.

Cheyenne sips her coffee. Like a dandelion,

apprehension has sprouted between them, veiled in disguise as they communicate, lightly dancing around the issue that is sure to come up.

Malcolm puts down his fork, wipes his mouth with a cloth napkin and sips at his coffee. Cheyenne watches him carefully.

"You know, baby," he says, "there's something I want us to discuss—or finish discussing."

"Okay." Cheyenne sets down her mug and gives him her full attention.

"What happened in New York really bothered me."

"I know." Cheyenne reaches out to stroke his forearm.

"What bothers me more than the incident itself—this stranger talking and touching you in a way that was . . ." Malcolm struggles to find the right word, "*intimate*—was the way you refused to tell me who and what he was, or *is* to you."

Cheyenne nods.

"I mean, come on—it was obvious to everyone in that church that you knew him—you said, he's an old friend. Well, yeah, that wasn't hard to figure out."

"Malcolm—"

"Wait—and here he is calling you 'Jazz.' Like 'pookie' or 'baby'—your own cute little nickname. Isn't that nice?" Malcolm exclaims.

"Malcolm," Cheyenne says, a bit louder this

time, "I told you he was an old friend. What more do I need to say? Come on, Mal—every time we go out, you are running into this person or that person, most of whom I've never even met, yet alone *heard* of. You don't see me *tripping*, do you?"

"Tripping? That's what you think I'm doing?" He doesn't wait for her to answer. "And what has gotten into you? What happened to the woman I knew who rarely questioned me when I made a simple request of her?"

"Nothing's gotten into me, Malcolm. I just don't know what to say that will please you. You want details about someone who I haven't even *thought* about in more than two decades." Cheyenne sighs, hoping Malcolm cannot detect her perjury. "Why do you refuse to drop this?" she asks.

"Simple. Because you aren't telling me shit!"

"I've already told you . . ."

"Stop!" Malcolm blares as he holds up his palm, jolting Cheyenne with his intensity. "I'm sick and tired of your bullshit, Cheyenne—you haven't told me anything! You say he's just a friend. Well, tell me this—what was he to you? Someone who calls my wife Jazz is more than just a friend, if you ask me!"

"I've told you—he was a friend, nothing more."

"Bullshit!" Malcolm's fist slams onto the

table, sending the plate of his half eaten omelet onto the stone deck. Cheyenne, jolted, backs away and stands, a look of shock twisted about her face. "You think I'm stupid," Malcolm says, rising from his chair, his finger pointed at Cheyenne. "You think I'm naïve. Let me tell you something, missy—I am none of those things. I'm your husband. And until four days ago—I thought I knew you. I thought I knew who you were and what you were about. I thought you were about being open and honest with me, but all of that has changed since *he* waltzed back into your life." Malcolm pauses and wipes at his mouth with his sleeve. His eyes are mere slits. He is seething.

"I thought I knew you, Cheyenne—but I don't. Perhaps you think that this new you can continue to come and go, hiding details of your life from me, but I'm here to tell you that you can't. You won't. I'm putting a stop to it right the fuck *now*."

Cheyenne has regained some of her nerve as she stares uncomprehendingly at her husband.

"Do you know what this is about, Malcolm? Do you?" she asks, as she kneels to collect the broken shards of the plate. "I'll tell you—it's about Malcolm not getting his way this time, not having his pretty little wife giving him the precise answer he craves so he can go on with his life, not having to worry about life *before* Malcolm. That's right—life before I met *you*." She tosses the plate pieces haphazardly onto the table. Malcolm stares at her wild-eyed as if she just committed a felony.

"And do you want to know why my old friend, Taj, yeah he has a name, why Taj calls me Jazz? I'll tell you, oh husband of mine. It's nothing mystical or romantic. Nothing clandestine or top secret—it's simple, really," Cheyenne says, emitting a short laugh, her stare never wavering from him.

"I used to sing for him. And he called me Jazz because he said the name suited me, that's all. No code word for 'time to hit it' or anything like that. Sorry."

"You fucked him." It was a statement, not a question.

"What I did before I met you is none of your business." She pauses for effect. "But for the record, no, I didn't fuck him."

"You're a liar," Malcolm hisses.

"Fuck you, Malcolm," Cheyenne says, turning to leave. Malcolm grabs her wrist before she has moved two feet.

"Get the hell off of me, Malcolm!" she yells.

"No, I won't—not until you come clean and tell me the god-damned truth—you fucked him—I can feel it."

"You're crazy—get off of me before I call the

police." She reaches out to grab at his arm, a feeble attempt to remove his hand from hers. He twists her arm, forcing her to cry out.

"Goddamn it, you're hurting me, Malcolm!" Cheyenne makes a fist and pumps it into his chest. Malcolm pushes her away and she slams into the doorframe.

"Admit it—you fucked him and that's why when you saw him you shed tears of joy," he shouts, his finger raised to her face. "What a . . ." He falters, searching for the right words.

"A what, Malcolm? What am I!?" Cheyenne shouts.

He opens his mouth slowly and says quietly: "I thought I knew you, Cheyenne. I thought I was the only one." He shakes his head miserably. "Well, the truth is finally revealed.

"So tell me Cheyenne, was it *that* good? Did Taj fuck you so damn good that it would bring you to tears? I guess so . . ." Malcolm's voice trails off.

"You are insane," she hisses, her hand covering her mouth.

"I guess we now know why you've been unable to produce a child. Old Taj must have fucked you so long and so hard, he left you damaged and barren inside."

CRACK!

Cheyenne's hand flies up as if powered by hydraulics and a mind of its own. She slaps him, connecting her palm against the flatness of his cheek. The sound of her slap reverberates off the deck and is carried by the morning breeze onward to the canyon valley.

Malcolm is stunned. His face registers the shock—he opens his mouth, but no words emerge. He backs up, holding his bruised face in his hand. His eyes are glassy, like the surface of a quiet lake at dawn, undisturbed.

Cheyenne stares at him incredulously, her lips trembling.

He opens the door that leads to the interior of their home and steps through. He turns to Cheyenne who remains immobile, tears cascading from her eyes.

"Now we know," Malcolm repeats, still holding his bruised face in hand, shutting the door quietly behind him.

Nine

Taj is upstairs when he hears the lock turning.

Shit.

She comes in, places her keys and purse on the walnut side table in the hallway, and shouts: "Baby! You here?"

Before he responds she is ascending the creaky stairs to his bedroom. She enters and sees his suitcase split open, half filled, with clothes spread around the bed.

Nicole frowns. "What's going on?" she asks incredulously.

"I was going to call you," Taj responds, a look of suffering touching the lines around his temples and cheeks.

"And say what?" she asks, standing at the entrance to the bedroom, arms folded, not wishing to proceed any further.

"Have a seat, Nicole," he offers warmly.

"Where? Your suitcase and clothes are everywhere." Nicole's head is shaking.

"I was going to call you," he repeats, walking over to her and taking her hand. "And tell you that I'm leaving."

"Going where?"

"This thing, Nikki, that's been *affecting* me," he pauses to consider all things that have transpired during the past week, "it's gotten to the point where I need to take control."

"And?" she says, her patience wearing thin.

"So I need to go take care of something. Wrap this mess up, once and for all."

"Okay, but you still haven't answered my question. Where are you going?" Nicole says.

"Jamaica."

"Jamaica? What's there? Oh—let me guess? *Her*." Nicole spins away from Taj and heads for the stairs.

"Nikki—wait!" Taj reaches for her shoulder. She turns.

"What? You expect me to stay here and listen to this? I don't think so."

"Nikki—it's not what you think! I'm not going to meet her or be with her. I'm going there . . ." He pauses to rub his head and frown. "How do I explain this? I'm going there to resolve, to bring closure to this thing that has haunted me for a long, long time. Longer than you know." His hazel eyes are turned down and for the first time, Nicole is scared.

She exhales slowly and walks back into the bedroom. She leans against the wall, and then slides down until she's resting on the thick carpet. Nicole looks great in her jeans, black boots, and a thick off-white sweater that accentuates her rich skin. For a moment, Taj wishes he could put all of this mess behind him and go back to the way things used to be.

That's not possible now.

Taj takes a seat beside her and lays his palm on her thigh. "Listen, Nikki—this is not a vacation for me. It's something I have to do."

"I understand. But, Taj—Jamaica? You haven't told me anything of what's going on. You aren't explaining to me why you have to go, what's down there, or why now all of a sudden you feel compelled to take this action."

"Nikki—it's not that simple. You expect me to lay this out for you, like one of your college lesson plans. Well, I can't do that. I don't understand all of the nuances myself. I just know that I have to do this—if I don't, this thing will continue to haunt me and I won't get past it. *We* won't get past it."

Nicole stares at him, processing the words.

"Taj—it's a week until Christmas. Do you realize that?"

"Yes, I know."

"How long will you be down there? Will you be back by then?

"Honestly, I don't know," he says. "A few days minimum, perhaps longer."

"So what am I supposed to do? We were planning on spending Christmas together. What am I supposed to do about that?"

Taj is silent, his head in his hands.

"Tell me the truth, Taj—are you going to see her? Just answer me that. Truthfully."

"The truth, Nikki—no. I don't even know where she is or how to contact her. No, I'm not doing this for her, I'm doing it for me."

Taj turns away and Nicole feels herself shiver. It's as if she has been dropped into a deep, black hole; she's falling, and then hits bottom with a resounding thunk.

"So, I'm supposed to let my fiancé run off to Jamaica to settle some score that's plagued him since long ago—I'm supposed to just go on with my life and hope things work out for the best?"

"Come on, Nikki—it's not like that."

"That's exactly what it is," she says, swatting his hand off her thigh and standing up. She glares down at him.

"It comes down to this—you and I are *supposed* to be getting married—you and I are *supposed* to be way past things like this—me wondering what you are up to, me wondering who this woman is who suddenly and mysteriously enters our lives. You and I are *supposed* to be communicating like man and wife . . ." Nicole shakes her head sadly. "But we're not."

Taj stands and goes to her. He wraps his arms around her waist and hugs her. Nicole's hands are at her sides.

"Baby—I don't know what else to say—I love you, you know that—I'm not using this as an excuse to do something I shouldn't or to run away. I'm doing this because I have to." He pulls her chin up with his hand. "Do you understand? I have to do this."

Nicole stares back. She blinks and nods once.

"Yes, Taj, I do."

She gently removes his hands and walks toward the door. At the doorframe she turns before heading down the stairs.

"You and I need to reevaluate what we have. And where we are going, Taj. I need to figure out if marriage is what is best for me, given these circumstances." There are tears in her eyes as she says this.

"Go do what you have to do, Taj, and be safe . . ."

"Wait—Nikki—please! This is not what I want!"

As he says this, his eye begins to quiver. He reaches up swiftly to quell the tremor.

But Nicole doesn't witness this.

She is already gone.

Ten

*T*he impenetrable jade canopy of trees below was Taj's only friend. It comforted him to see greenery from the porthole, so he pressed his face against the glass and held it there, tightly. For the moment, it calmed him.

Cheyenne remained in her seat.

Her mother had dragged herself back and into a seat a few rows ahead, too exhausted and in pain to move any further. She barked for Cheyenne to stay put.

And Cheyenne obeyed.

The screams had subsided, now replaced with quiet sobs. Taj was sick to his stomach, intensely embarrassed over his inability to do anything other than sit still and puke.

Sit still and puke.

What else could he possibly do? Wrestle with the crazed Seifu? Fly the plane?

No.

Every few moments Taj attempted to raise his gaze above the leather seats and stare into the cockpit, to see what was going on. He even nudged Cheyenne with his elbow, his first time speaking to her.

"Can you see anything up there? What's going on?" he whispered, cognizant of his vomit breath on her face.

"No," she said quietly, shaking her head, but not looking at him. "I have no idea what is happening..."

Taj went back to pressing his face against the glass, hoping this was all a bad dream, that any moment he would wake from this horrific slumber, startled, yet conscious, and laugh with the realization that it all had been a terrible, dreadful delusion.

For a moment, he believed that it really could be the figment of his imagination—that he had conjured up all of this stuff*—Seifu and his black cane, the buffeting of the airplane as it lost control, Cheyenne's heart-wrenching screams, and her mother being knocked around like a sheet of newsprint on a windy day.*

That maybe, just maybe, everything that had happened was not real. The plane seemed to be flying level once again. Perhaps he had been perplexed by the nausea—that in reality, nothing bad had happened—and they were going to be okay.

AWAKENING

Taj sneaked a peek at Cheyenne who was dazed and confused—staring straight ahead, breathing rapidly, her gaze unblinking. He took his hand, wiped it against his pants before gingerly placing it on her arm. Turning, he said to her, "It'll be okay."

Cheyenne glanced at him and smiled weakly.

Was it possible that he imagined all of this?

No, it wasn't possible.

Cheyenne's frightened look said it all.

The sound of the engines changed, a low-pitched drone, and that brought Taj out of his quizzical state. His stare flew to the porthole as he felt the plane's altitude change—the nose dipping down. Then he saw it. The canopy was creeping closer.

Fear tightened around his lungs, making it difficult to breathe.

Then the sound stopped.

The engines shut down.

First the left. Then the right.

And all Taj could hear was the whistling of the wings through the air.

The nose dipped some more, and Taj felt himself free falling, like that roller coaster ride at Great Adventure that Pop had taken him to. Except this was no amusement park ride.

He saw a clearing off in the distance—a reddish-brown tract of land that was devoid of trees. He felt the plane shudder as it dropped, way too fast in Taj's estimation. The wings seemed to move with the wind, like wings on a seagull, flapping in a way that Taj prayed was an illusion.

The plane tipped to the right, nose still down, the howling of the wind increasing to almost a scream.

Cheyenne was wide-eyed and frantic. Her mother was calling for Seifu from the confines of her seat. Seifu returned no response.

The plane leveled as Taj took in the tops of trees that seemed much too close to the wings.

"Jesus!" he exclaimed.

Cheyenne's head snapped toward him, but he said nothing further. His hands gripped both arm-rests, the nauseous feeling rising within.

The trees were coming closer. He could now discern branches and treetops. He had lost sight of the clearing. He scanned out the porthole for it, hoping to use it as a reference point, to assist in orientation.

A landing zone. Taj prayed to God that it was.

His thought was interrupted. The plane dipped again, branches reaching up to tickle the belly of the Beech King Air.

A disturbing, arresting sound abruptly filled the cabin. Taj could only watch in horror as the air-frame collided with the canopy, wings dipping into the thick treetops as if they were wispy clouds.

Suddenly they were twisting and turning; gut-wrenching groans emitted from the Beech King as the wings snapped off like twigs. Taj didn't have time to scream.

No one did.

AWAKENING

They were falling through the thick, dark woodland to the forest floor below, the Beech King disintegrating as they went.

Plunging into darkness as they dropped.

Obscure shadows consuming them.

Then only the stillness of darkness . . .

Eleven

Air Jamaica utlizes a fleet of modern jets, mostly 767s—wide-body airplanes with huge Pratt and Whitney engines, modern avionics, and luxury seats. The jet sitting on the tarmac at Baltimore Washington International is easily five to six times the size of a puddle jumper; its shell gleams in the morning sun as workers fill the jet with luggage and fuel.

Seeing the beast does nothing to allay Taj's fears. He stares at the thing as if it were an alien being—something not of this world—and he is immensely frightened.

No, frightened isn't the appropriate word. Unrestrained terror courses through every vein of Taj's body. He is vibrating and on fire. Taj hasn't been on a plane in decades. But today, he has no choice.

AWAKENING

Taj walks to a water fountain and bends down to take a sip. He slips a Valium into his mouth and swallows, hoping relief will come quickly.

He finds a seat in the lounge away from the others—vacationers, unlike him, wearing broad smiles and dressed in bright prints and sandals, even though it's thirty degrees outside. A week before Christmas. They are heading to an island paradise where the air is seventy-eight degrees, the jerk chicken and reggae music are to die for, and the natives are friendly. Why wouldn't they be smiling?

Taj attempts to read a *USA Today* that he has found abandoned in the adjacent seat. He flips through the pages, his mind on autopilot, not paying attention to the stories or even capturing the essence of the content; his eyes scan the words only—they are mere letters that are processed and discarded, nothing more.

He is anxious.

Taj knows the statistics like most folks—air travel is safe—the number of plane crashes is way down. And with added security, the potential of a terrorist threat is minimal. Air Jamaica, he is sure, has never had a fatality.

But that doesn't change what Taj knows.

It can happen.

It happened to *him*.

An announcement indicating that they will begin boarding soon slices through his concentration. Taj gathers his things and feels his

93

chest walls constricting. His heart is pounding so loudly that he is afraid others may hear it, too. He glances around but no one is paying him any mind.

At the gate, Taj hands his boarding pass to the attendant, his legs moving autonomously, as he heads down the walkway. At the door he smiles weakly at a striking Jamaican woman who welcomes him with an engaging beam. He takes his seat by the window, feeling the Valium begin to wash through him, a gentle wave that caresses and soothes.

Taj closes his eyes and recites a silent prayer: Make this flight a safe one. Get him to his destination in one piece and home again without complication. And let him free himself of the vile demons that have remained hidden away, chained to his psyche, waiting for the opportune moment to emerge.

This time, Taj prays his God is listening . . .

Cheyenne's cell phone has been ringing incessantly. She has lost track of just how many times over the past few days. She has come to hate the thing. And she wonders what people did before the damned contraption?

Malcolm has been calling and texting almost non-stop since their fight three days ago. From the house, from his office, and from his cell. In the mornings, afternoons, and evenings.

Especially in the evenings—and late into the evening. It's as if his guilt complex shifts into overdrive after dinnertime as he sits alone in their regal home, grieving and wondering just where she is and—most importantly—with *whom*?

She will not give him the satisfaction of answering or even returning a single call.

He's left messages—too numerous to recall. All with the singular theme of "I'm so sorry."

Cheyenne is not moved. She has turned the phone off, turned it back on, left it on vibrate for hours at a time, until that buzzing noise made her insane. She knows the effect that turning her phone off has on Malcolm—he hates it when a call goes directly to voice mail. He's commented about it all the time.

"What the fuck's the use of having a cell," Malcolm is fond of opining, "if they don't keep the damned thing on?"

She has to give Malcolm credit. Her husband is slick. He first began attempting to track her whereabouts days ago. When that didn't work he broke down and called her close girlfriends, knowing that they would immediately call her to see if she was okay. All Malcolm would then have to do is wait an hour or so and then call the girlfriends back to get the 411.

However, that plan was a non-starter because Cheyenne wasn't responding to her girlfriends' calls either. She wasn't taking anyone's calls. And she didn't have any family left to speak of, so he couldn't call them. Malcolm was shit out of luck.

Cheyenne lounges in an oversized striped chaise in her hotel room. She wears jeans and a cardigan sweater over a comfortable top. She wears no makeup. She doesn't have to. That's one thing that Malcolm used to comment on—the fact that she, unlike most women, possessed natural beauty. She could wake up, simply wash her face, and come out looking radiant. He had always loved that about her.

She is in a nice hotel about an hour and a half from home. Money's not an issue. She has plenty of credit cards and access to the bank accounts from her phone. Rather than going home to collect her things she went shopping two days ago and spent a few grand on what she needed—shoes, jeans, tops, a loose-fitting leather jacket, toilet articles, and luggage. Nothing fancy, but quality stuff.

She has been eating at a variety of establishments a short drive away from the hotel or utilizing room service, allowing her palate to be well stimulated. She works out at the hotel gym every day, takes a swim, and catches up on her reading. She bought some CDs and listens to old school music.

Cheyenne is doing okay. Ever since she slapped Malcolm and left him, Cheyenne has felt a steady surge of inner strength. Now she is far less anxious.

The cell phone rings—breaking her out of the daze that has enveloped her like a fog.

Right on schedule, like clockwork.

Her first reaction is to let it ring, like all the others. But then she thinks about this strategy, and nods at its flaws. Obviously, she needs to talk to him sooner or later—has to get the conversation over—inevitably.

It might as well be now.

She reaches for the phone and answers it. Hears Malcolm's obvious surprise.

"Yes," she says cordially.

"Baby. Damn—I can't believe you finally answered—I've been going crazy worrying about you."

"I'm alive, Malcolm. No broken bones. Only my insides are bruised, especially my heart. But I'll live."

"Baby I'm so sorry for what I said."

Silence.

"Baby—I had no right to say what I did. That was way out of line—shit, baby—where are you?"

"A hotel."

"Which one?"

"It doesn't matter, Malcolm."

A pause as if he's maneuvering over land-mines.

"And—are you alone?"

This sets Cheyenne off.

"No, Malcolm, I've got half the fucking L.A. Lakers with me and we just finished a marathon fuck session!"

"Baby, I'm sorry—it's just that when you didn't come home or return my calls . . ."

"What Malcolm?" she interrupts, her anger clearly evident. "You just assumed that I shacked up with him—that I was just waiting for the opportunity to run out and get fucked, is that it?"

"Cheyenne, calm down," he says pensively.

"No, Malcolm, I will not calm down. It is you who needs to calm down. You've turned into this . . . *person* . . . who is out of control. And I neither like it nor will I tolerate it."

"I'm sorry" is all he can say.

There are several seconds of quiet while both Cheyenne and Malcolm think about what comes next. Malcolm ruptures the silence.

"Baby—come home. Please."

"No, Malcolm. It's not that simple."

"But why?"

"Because you hurt me—more than you know."

"I know, and I am sorry. But staying away from me is not going to fix anything. You need to come home so that we can work this out—together."

Cheyenne can hear the pleading in his voice.

"Malcolm—I'm not coming home—not now. I don't know when. You have to understand something—you really hurt me. Your words were vile and cut straight to the bone. You said exactly what you've been thinking and feeling all of these years—and frankly, I need time to digest all of this."

"Cheyenne," Malcolm says, "baby—I think you are making . . ." Here he pauses as if to search for the right word, and she can hear the phrase, *big deal* forming on his lips. Instead he continues, "an issue out of a single incident. You and I have been together for a long time—we don't fight that much—this is the first major incident we've had."

She hollers, "And that's why you don't get why I am acting this way due to a single incident. The point, Malcolm, is not whether this is the first time or the seventeenth. The fact, Malcolm, is that you said it to me and you meant it—it shows me *clearly* what you think of me and our marriage."

"Wait a second, that's not—"

"Let me finish! You called me, remember? You know what this entire charade says to me about you Malcolm? It says that you fundamentally don't trust me. Furthermore, you have this vision of me as a lily-white virgin princess who did not exist before you arrived. Well, I'm here to tell you—I had a life before you. Yeah, Malcolm, we don't talk about it much—because I see how it bruises your pride. But you did not make me a woman, Malcolm. I was a woman *before* I met you!"

Cheyenne is up and pacing about the room, the octave of her voice rising like the Pacific tides.

"What is *that* supposed to mean?"

"It means what it means. Look, I'm not going to argue with you. I'm not ready to come home now—not yet. I don't know when I will be ready, because I need some more time to sort through all of my feelings."

"So," Malcolm says, the air deflated from his sails, "you're going to live out of a suitcase for what? A few days, a week?"

"Yeah, perhaps more. I'm going to take the time I need. And I suggest, for the sake of our marriage, that you respect my decision and let me work through this—*alone.*"

There is a long silence as Malcolm ponders Cheyenne's words. He is angry, hurt, inflamed, bruised, and most notably, misses his wife. At the same time, he's trying his best to not make an already bad situation any worse.

"Baby, is that your final answer?" he chuckles softly.

"Yeah, Malcolm, it is."

"And what about Christmas? What am I supposed to do?"

"I'm sorry, Malcolm, but I didn't put us in this predicament—you did!" Cheyenne winces as soon as the words escape her lips because she knows she's been unduly hard on him.

Good. Perhaps he'll think long and hard about what he said . . .

"Okay." Malcolm is silent. Moments pass on the phone—dead space as their respective minds whirl. "I guess I will talk to you soon," he says.

"Yeah."

"Take care," he says, almost a whisper. "One more thing, Cheyenne, before I go."

"Yes?"

"I now know why he called you Jazz . . ."

"What? What are you talking about? I told you why."

"I know you did," Malcolm says, "but that's not the real reason. I've figured it out." He does not wait for Cheyenne to interject. "A long time ago, right before we made love for the very first time you showed me your tattoo. I remember stroking your thigh and asking you about the flower."

Cheyenne's breathing is arrested.

"You told me it wasn't just any old flower, but a particular flower called jasmine. I had forgotten about that since it happened so long ago, but I recalled it the other day."

Malcolm swallows hard before continuing.

"That's why he called you Jazz. Because of the tattoo. Not because you used to sing for him. Not for any other reason."

Cheyenne hears the phone go dead. She stands there, at the window, glancing down at the outdoor pool, which is empty. There are petite waves that reflect stray moonlight. The scene is haunting, yet beautiful.

She is mute. The phone slips silently from her hand and falls to the carpet.

Malcolm, she reflects, has it mostly right.

Twelve

The takeoff roll is smooth into the brisk, clear morning. Taj has willed himself to be calm—he controls his breathing by imagining each breath as long thin tendrils of smoke that enter and exit his body, invading and filling his lungs and capillaries before retreating. He sees this in his mind: the columns of air are like soldiers marching off to battle, each one in step and in tune to the one beside the other; it quiets him and makes him tranquil.

The plane is half full. Taj does not have anyone else in his row. For this he is immensely grateful.

The jet arcs over the Eastern Shore, the imposing Chesapeake Bay Bridge, and Annapolis, the capital of Maryland, before heading south. His nerves are composed, thanks to the

Valium. Nevertheless, they remain coiled up and ready, like a cobra about to strike should the need arise.

Taj remembers that the other plane ride many years ago began this same way: a smooth takeoff, gliding into the sky and suspended above the clouds as an angel. But then things got out of control and went bad—very, very bad, and . . .

Stop it. Things will be different this time.

Taj watches a short video on Jamaica produced by her ministry of tourism. The images are soothing and inviting: seductive beaches, pulsating music, rich history. Taj is intrigued and temporarily overlooks his present situation. He glances at his wristwatch—three and a half hours. He views the timepiece as a countdown timer—T minus three and a half hours to go. He hopes the trip will go fast. With any luck, all will be well and he will land safely in no time.

From the seat back screen in front of him, Taj selects a movie on this flight—a film called *Serendipity* with John Cusack that Taj has not heard of or seen. He watches the preview: two people who meet during a Christmas shopping spree and spend a short evening together. There are sparks flying between them, but they part company before they find out where it will lead. Ten years later, both immersed in relationships, they put true love to the test by reuniting—but they have to find each other first . . .

The small screen is mesmerizing to Taj. The storyline is hauntingly similar. He puts on his ear buds, lowers his shade, and plunges headlong into the movie.

An hour later, the plane begins to buffet from turbulence. The pilot comes on to say that they will be experiencing some light chop—that is what he calls it—for the next thirty minutes or so. Taj raises the shade to glance out. A sea of unbroken clouds lies beneath them. They are somewhere south of Charleston, hugging the coastline as they fly toward Cuba. Taj rises from his seat and heads to the rest room, a look of panic set upon his smooth face. He splashes water on his skin as air rocks the plane, both horizontally and vertically. Taj holds himself in the tiny restroom as he senses the nausea building deep inside of him. The feelings and emotions return—hard not to given the conditions—and he is suddenly transported back to his youth of twenty years ago and the Beech King Air with its white fuselage and red and black trim. He remembers it standing almost defiantly on the smoldering tarmac of Norman Manley International in the unbearable afternoon sun.

That was before it fell from the sky.

And that wasn't the worst of it . . .

Stop it.

Taj splashes his face again, then glances up and gawks at the face staring back at him in reflection. He wills himself to calm down. This trip, unlike the other, will end landing safely and out of harm's way.

Taj will not allow himself to slip into the abyss—that dank dark place where demons dwell. Demons who make him recall horrific things. Things that he hasn't thought about or dreamed of for decades.

Taj and Cheyenne made a pact. They vowed to be silent, move on with their lives and be okay. Taj intends to keep his part of the bargain.

Exiting the restroom, he almost collides with an attractive flight attendant—the one who had welcomed him aboard earlier.

She notices his ashen features and reaches out to stroke his arm.

"Are you okay, sir?"

"I'm fine," Taj responds, embarrassed to say anything further.

"First time flying?" she asks, a genuine smile adorning her face.

Taj thinks. "No, not really."

"These things do this every once in a while—no need to feel nervous." Taj assumes she is referring to the turbulence. "May I get you anything? Something refreshing perhaps to calm your nerves?"

AWAKENING

Taj stares at her—she has such a youthful face. It is smooth, black, and so wonderfully vibrant that when she smiles, she soothes. Her eyes widen and her cheekbones rise making him feel warm and cozy. He wants to tell her what he's feeling—wants so badly to spill this thing that has been inside of him for so long. Taj desperately wants to rid himself of this *stuff* that is poisoning him.

Instead, he smiles weakly, shakes his head, and says: "No thank you, I'm going to be all right." Taj shuffles back to his seat hoping to lose himself in the rest of the movie . . .

He thinks about Cheyenne, wonders if she is thinking about him this very instant. In fact, he wonders has she thought about him even once since their chance encounter in New York? An instance that seems so long ago.

Taj wonders how things would be different if he had never run into her again. He'd be home in Washington, Nicole on his arm, preparing for the holidays, wrapping presents, waiting until the last minute to trim the tree, as was the custom with his family. And the demons would have remained buried, out of sight, out of reach.

Cheyenne, he bets, is probably home right now doing those things that he longs to do—with her husband, and perhaps her child or children—not wondering about him or what was he doing this moment . . . not having the time or the inclination to think about him or their chance meeting that altered his world.

Everything happened so quickly. Last night, Cheyenne remained standing by the window for what seemed like an hour—glancing down at the pool, staring at the waves—losing herself amidst the alternating patterns of darkness and light—the cell phone laying untouched on the carpet by her ankle—thinking about Malcolm's last words—those words that cut to the bone, like a sharp blow to the face.

Malcolm knew. He *knew*.

And then, like a quick snap of the neck, she shattered the trance that held her and moved to action. Her first task was to call the concierge. Yes it was late, but she needed some answers.

Cheyenne asked for a list of flights leaving within the next forty-eight hours. There was nothing direct, but she could get a non-stop in the morning to Miami and fly on to Montego Bay that afternoon. Cheyenne gave the concierge her credit card number and told her to book the flight.

She called a handful of close friends to tell them what was happening. She didn't say where she was going or for how long, just that she would not be home for the holiday. And

yes, she knew that Malcolm was calling relent-
lessly looking for her—she was fine and would
be all right.

She packed around one and slept for less
than four hours. A car would be waiting for
her at seven.

This was crazy, what she was doing—she
should be going home to her husband, a man
with flaws but someone who loved her. And
she loved him back.

But something told her that now was the
time to do what she needed to do. This
thought had been swimming in and out of
focus for a long time—hovering in the background like noise. She knew it was there, but
never paid it any mind—until that fateful
evening in New York when she saw *him* again.

Cheyenne knew she had to finish this once
and for all. It wasn't about him. It was about
her.

The hotel checkout, drive to the airport,
check in, and security screening was one long
colorful blur, like a movie that whizzes past
your senses (or an amusement park ride that's
invigorating and exhausting simultaneously),
until Cheyenne found herself in an aisle seat
on a plane bound for Jamaica. To settle a
score.

She sits there now, the plane rising into the
morning sky, heading east, to a place she hasn't

been since she was young, so many years ago. She is afraid.

Not of what she will find. But of the thoughts and emotions that will be dredged up by traveling there. She, like Taj, has sealed up that chapter of her life—closing it and battening it down until not even a wisp of memories emerged.

She had killed them, stabbed and gored them repeatedly until they no longer breathed—and she could once again sleep at night without waking up screaming . . .

Those nights seemed so long ago to her. She now allows herself the time to whisk back to that time and to concentrate on his face—the only thing that got her through her ordeal. It calmed her, and made her see past herself.

It helped her grow. Mostly, it kept her alive. So now, she allows herself to do what she has been unable to do since she heard those words that sent a chill down the nape of her neck: "Jazz, look into my eyes . . ."

She remembers.

She remembers him in all of his glorious and vivid detail. Those arresting eyes. The youthful dark face—handsome and rugged in a sensual way. Hands that attempted to shield her from harm's way.

And failed.

Cheyenne recalls seeing him for the first

time on the commuter plane, as he bent down to enter the cabin—he was tall even then. Their eyes met briefly, but honestly, she paid him no mind. Not then.

Not until the ordeal began.

Cheyenne's stomach begins to twist violently, as if there is something living inside her. She orders rum and Coke to soothe her nerves, and wishes that she had something stronger. Cheyenne sips the drink and closes her eyes, tipping her head back as the liquid washes down her throat, warming her insides, and calming her nerves.

She wonders where he is now. Where does he live? What does he do? She wishes that they could speak again—for more than a brief moment—engage each other so that they could finish what began long ago and has remained unresolved all of these years.

Sweet Taj.

Cheyenne shakes her head. She thinks of Malcolm and she feels regret—because she knows she is hurting him—for the things that she has said and has yet to do.

But this journey is something that must be done.

Malcolm will be all right. He'll get through this.

Shifting gears, she wonders if she had the opportunity to speak to Taj once again—to see his lovely face—what would she say? What

111

would she do if she found herself face to face with him once again?

The question shames her. There are unhealthy thoughts that bob to the surface like a cork. She shakes her head again—it is so much more than some kind of raw physical need, a thirst that must be quenched. This is so much more than that.

Would they even be able to say much after the first few minutes? What would her contribution be to the dialogue?"

"So, Taj—you married, divorced, single, or what?"

"Where do you make your home these days?"

"Are you happy, Taj?"

"Did you learn to forget about me, Taj—or in the stillness of the night, does my face still haunt you, like yours does me?"

Finishing the drink, Cheyenne knows that it really doesn't matter. The questions will go unanswered—most probably forever. She will never see him again—the odds of finding each other are very small or damn near nil, not in this great expanse of a world.

She could improve the odds by trying to find him. But she's not going to do that. She's going to leave Taj alone.

It's better that way.

Thirteen

*H*e awakened with a jolt—a feeling that shocked
and frightened him. He opened his eyes but
saw only darkness. He was listing badly to one side,
and felt trapped. Immediately, his entire body ached.
His face was on fire—he reached for it—felt it sticky
and bruised. Touched a finger to his lips and tasted
blood.

Taj moved his head to the side. Darkness enveloped him like a thick blanket. His mind raced—
where the hell am I? What happened to me?

And the sudden realization came crashing down
on him.

He had been in a plane crash!

Was he alive?

Taj was sure that he was. But he couldn't see.

Did that mean he was blind?

His hands went to his face and eyes, but couldn't
detect any major damage.

He wrestled to free himself. He was somehow bound to his seat.

Taj yelled. "Can anyone hear me?"

Silence.

Okay, calm down—take stock of the situation first.

You're not dead.

You can't see.

Why is that?

It could be because it is dark.

Taj concentrated on his surroundings. He ceased firing instructions that were flying around inside his head at light speed, and allowed himself to just listen.

He listened intently.

And he heard the sounds of the jungle.

Soft, at first, but then noticeably discernible— buzzing sounds, creaking noises, off-in-the-distant groans, animal sounds. He twisted his head to focus his hearing.

A crackling sound—low pitched and seemingly far away—like a fire. He sniffed—and for the first time was aware of the smell—a burning odor and a faint whiff of something else—oil or jet fuel—he couldn't be sure.

Taj reached to the right where the porthole was— and his hand waved through the air. He reached down and immediately connected with the jagged metal. It cut his hand and he cried out in pain.

Wincing, he suddenly remembered the girl, Cheyenne, who had been seated next to him. He shifted his gaze to the left, still couldn't see anything, and leaned toward her. He reached out and connected with a shoulder.

He probed the flesh while he spoke.

"Hey, are you okay? Are you awake? Wake up!"

He probed harder, and felt her leg. She shifted slightly with his touch and then moaned.

Taj felt a surge of hope and adrenaline race through his veins.

She was alive, too.

He began shaking her, as best as he could, seeing how he was immobile in his seat and listing away from her. Just shifting and reaching for her was difficult, exhausting work, and he tired easily.

More moans from her.

"Can you hear me?"

A weak response, "Where am I?"

Taj shifted closer. "Can you hear me? We're still on the plane, I think." He found her hand, closed his fingers over hers and felt her squeeze.

"Open your eyes, if you can—tell me if you can see."

A moment passed. "No," she croaked. Taj's hand remained holding hers. "Mamma, where are you?" She tried to raise her voice but it only caused her to cough violently. Taj felt her body tense.

No response. The girl began to sob loudly. She cried out repeatedly for her mother.

Still nothing.

"Hey—it's going to be all right," he said, attempting to offer what little moral support he could *muster.* "Listen—I think it's nighttime, which is why we can't see—we need to sit tight and wait for the light to come."

Taj thought about his surroundings. He had no idea where they had landed. They could be anywhere, and the condition of the plane, without seeing it, was completely unknown.

He didn't even know his overall condition or that of the girl's. And since he had not heard a word from Seifu, the girl's mom, or the pilot, it was too early to guess at their fate.

Taj felt exhausted. He sat back, holding the girl's hand and repeated to himself and to her: "Everything's going to be okay."

The sky softened. Taj, who had been drifting in and out of consciousness, finally noticed it. It was as if one minute it was pitch black outside and the next he could actually see shadows. The sky was turning a deep indigo, and Taj could hear that the night sounds had changed—as if the forest creatures knew of night's finish and began their retreat to their sanctuary to wait out the light that was sure to come. He twisted his head around to better take in his surroundings. Yes, he could discern shapes and shadows now. He could not tell where he was or what the shapes represented, but he definitely could see something.

He nudged Cheyenne with his hand.

"Are you awake? Can you hear me?"

"What?" It was a low moan.

"It's getting light—can you see it? I can see shadows. It should be light soon."

Turning to her, he reached for her hand and squeezed it. She squeezed lightly back. He fell back to sleep.

When he awoke it was still dark, but the sky had lightened sufficiently to the point where he could see better.

Taj and Cheyenne were in what remained of the cabin. It lay on its side, badly mangled in the midst of a tall forest. The cabin roof had collapsed and was mere inches from Taj's head. Only four rows of seats were intact—Taj's, the one behind him, and the two in front. The rest of the plane was gone.

Taj glanced over to Cheyenne. She was bloodied, like him, and slumped over to one side. He shook her and she awoke with a groan.

It took Taj some time to disengage from the seat-belt and extricate himself from the cabin seat. He next helped Cheyenne. They rested on the ground when they were free, their chests heaving from the exertion.

They both took stock of themselves. Miraculously, other than bruises and not-too-deep lacerations, they were unharmed. They could walk, thankfully, albeit weakly.

Cheyenne glanced around frantically.

"Where's the rest of the plane? Where is my mamma?"

Taj shook his head. "I don't know. It's not light enough to search—but we will."

They both sat on the ground, shivering from the cold. There wasn't much to say between them—they had just braved a plane crash—and lived.

What do you say to someone with whom you've just survived something horrific? Especially when the fate of the rest of the passengers and crew is unknown . . .

Silence is best.

The sun exploded over them at dawn, sending warming rays through the canopy to the forest below. The remains of the cabin had come to rest in a small clearing, the tall trees towering above them. It was difficult to look at the cabin, its distorted, mutilated fuselage, twisted and burned. Taj glanced around and was able to discern the trail that had taken them through the trees—some of the tops and branches were sheared off—others were burned black and still smoldering. A light haze hung in the air, the smell of jet fuel distinctly noticeable. Taj walked away from the wreckage, glancing upward as he tried to trace the path—and then he saw it. Only a few hundred yards away in the trees, thirty or so feet up, caught between thick branches and overgrown vines that held it like loving arms was the nose of the Beech King Air—the cockpit, or what was left of it—just a short white nub, the rest

118

cleaved off by God knows what. It had lodged in the thick foliage and come to rest hanging nose down.

Taj yelled for Cheyenne. She hobbled over, still too weak to run.

She saw the nosecone of the plane and her hand rushed to her face. She screamed for her mother, but again, received no response.

Taj ran to the base of the tree—glanced around frantically as if some tools and equipment would miraculously appear. When they did not, he silently began to climb.

It was a difficult task, climbing, his body aching, his face still on fire from his wounds. But Taj was in excellent shape—athletic. Not that he participated in high school sports, but he was the kind of kid who kept active and strong. His pop had seen to that.

He pulled himself up the first fifteen feet quickly and stopped to rest in the crook of two limbs. He stared down at Cheyenne who sat Indian style on the ground, eyeing the ruined cockpit, her face totally filled with the dread of someone who has just lost a loved one. At that moment Taj felt extreme pity for her—and that is what drove him on—perhaps there was someone alive up there. He climbed higher.

As he worked his way closer to what was left of the aircraft, he was thinking of Pop's work ethic. Whenever Taj found himself tired and paused to stop, thoughts of his pop rushed into his head—his fa-

ther wiping the sweat from his brow with a thick, dark forearm as he slung fresh fish onto a decaying dock—eyeing his boy curiously and telling him that this—his work—was all he had—and so he needed to do it right and not act shiftless.

From before sunup until after sundown (often fourteen to sixteen hours a day), his pop would work on the water, finally coming home stinking of fish—the smell ingrained into his skin and pores, under his fingernails, the stench trapped in his thick black hair. It was a smell reminiscent of the aftertaste of cigars, something not easily removed. His pop would remain in the shower for more than half an hour, but still would come out feeling as if he had not removed the smell.

If, by some means of communication, his pop were able to speak to him now, he'd tell Taj to haul his ass up that tree, and do whatever it takes to reach the cockpit. So, Taj continued to climb, mindful of the fact that the cockpit was in a precarious position—hanging, literally, by the good graces of only tree limbs, branches, and vines. At any time, suddenly succumbing to the effects of gravity, it could come crashing down onto his black little head.

Taj was feeling not like a hero or anything special—just a dazed and traumatized young boy who was operating on autopilot—placing one arm in front of the other and pulling his weary body upward. When he reached the cockpit, chunks of its metal skin flapping like a flag in the Jamaican breeze, he paused to take a breath. He cautiously peered into the shattered glass and vomited straight away.

The pilot was dead in the left seat. Taj recoiled from those eyes that stared back at him—vacant lifeless orbs that spoke little of the terror that befell their owner.

But that wasn't the worst part.

Across his neckline was a deep and jagged wound surrounded by congealed blood and ragged flesh. Someone had sliced his throat wide open.

That someone was Seifu, who sat in the right seat.

Whether he was dead or just unconscious, Taj couldn't tell, so he maneuvered around the broken hull and climbed higher. He reached the torn back of the cockpit, whose hydraulics and electrical lines had been hacked away in the violent impact. Taj glanced upward and around, trying in vain to locate the rest of the plane. Cheyenne's mother was nowhere to be seen.

A shudder went through the trees and what was left of the plane's nose. Taj heard faint laughter.

He bent down holding onto a thick branch for support, and glanced over at the cockpit window.

Seifu was staring at him and laughing . . .

Fourteen

Cheyenne is doing okay. The first few hours of her flight have passed without incident. She busies herself with reading—alternating between magazines and a Toni Morrison hardback purchased in the airport bookstore—and listening to her music. She wishes she could sing right now, open up her lungs and free herself the way she does when there's no one in the house; singing not only unwinds but calms her as well. She finds singing therapeutic, refreshing, and invigorating like a cleansing spring rain. But this can't happen here. A plane is not the place for singing.

The in-flight movie does not interest her. She glances outside her window, enjoying the gentle roll of the earth as they make their way steadily eastward. The mountains fascinate her with their sharp, snow-dusted peaks, dirty brown valleys, and angled depressions. She sees a lone road that snakes along, deserted, pencil thin from this height, and she wonders about folks who live down there, miles from the predilections of an urban sprawl. How wonderful it must be to be out among the elements and face-to-face with nature—raw and uncut, the unfiltered air that tastes like fresh, early morning dew.

She goes back to her reading and puts on another playlist—anything to keep her mind active. Until now she's done an excellent job of not thinking about what is just beneath the surface of her psyche, awaiting her like a fox about to pounce on its prey.

Cheyenne knows it is inevitable; the emotional floodgates are about to open—she can sense it coming. When it's ready to happen, she won't put up a fight or stand in its way, but she's not going to help it along.

She gets up to stretch her legs, runs her hands down the front of her jeans to press them, and excuses herself as she maneuvers by a passenger to reach the aisle. The aircraft is only half filled. She moves toward the back, observing the passengers as she goes. About half are watching the movie attentively. The rest are playing on their iPads or dozing. A few business travelers are tapping away on their laptops.

Cheyenne scans the faces in their seats. Some

are black, white, Asian, young, elderly; there's a woman shushing an infant child to sleep, and a family of four—taking up an entire row—the children tugging on some portable electronics device while the father and mother snore away, oblivious to the behavior of their offspring. She wonders if these people's lives are as complicated as hers? Could it be that they have issues that overwhelm them and keep them wide-awake and sweating at night?

Probably not.

Cheyenne is halfway to the back when she spots him. He's sitting by the window, the seats beside him vacant. His head is down, but the thick, dark dreadlocks are unmistakable.

Cheyenne's step falters.

At that moment, he glances up and stares at her. Their eyes lock—he smiles, and Cheyenne's face melts as the realization punches into her mid-section, like a bullet being fired, almost knocking her to the ground with its force.

It's Seifu.

The features—dark face and eyes; the evil, cynical smile created with bright teeth—are the same. He nods slowly as Cheyenne feels the plane begin to tip forward and nose down. She is instantly lightheaded and the sensation of falling is so great that she must reach out and grasp the seat backs to keep from toppling over.

Her breathing is immediately cut short. It's as if her windpipe is obstructed and only tiny puffs of air can get by.

A flight attendant comes up behind her and asks if she is okay. Cheyenne is silent.

It can't be Seifu. It is not possible. But he is here and his smile cannot be denied.

Her legs are jelly and are giving way. Seifu continues to stare at her—his eyes continue their lock. A wicked grin spreads across his face, as if she were jam and he intends to eat her, extending his tongue and devouring her sweetness. She is sickened to the point of complete exhaustion.

The flight attendant touches her shoulder and repeats the question. A few passengers look at her in fascination. When she doesn't respond, the attendant moves Cheyenne along toward the back. She staggers down the aisle as the flight attendant's voice soothes her, the only thing onto which she can grasp. They pass Seifu, and Cheyenne feels her skin bead up and prickle from sheer revulsion. His gaze follows her like a hawk.

"Is the young lady well?" he asks the attendant in a perfect British accent, and Cheyenne realizes in an instant that the man watching her is *not* Seifu.

Relief floods through her like a torrential river, as if the faucets of her soul have suddenly been opened; blood and oxygen are once again flowing, unencumbered. Cheyenne is led to an empty row a few seats behind the Seifu look-alike. She moves across the aisle (sitting behind him is not an option) and plunks down breathless and weary. The attendant is back in a flash with a glass of water, which Cheyenne immediately downs.

Her throat is on fire. The water squelches the flames.

She sits for a moment, regaining her strength and trying not to concentrate on what just occurred. A silly case of mistaken identity, that's all. No need to get upset. Calm down . . . keep it together.

The aircraft hits an air pocket and the plane dips momentarily. Cheyenne's hand attacks the armrest, bracing for the worst, as she is transported back to a short plane ride that began decades ago like this one.

Gasping helplessly in terror as Seifu does the unthinkable, unable to reach her mamma who lies crumpled on the floor upfront, and the violent changes in pitch and altitude as the Beech King Air falls to earth . . .

The plane buffets again, the seat belt sign illuminates, and Cheyenne feels herself losing control. The floodgates open and she begins her spiral down, like that of the Beech King Air, down into the muck and sticky mire of her mind, where hideous things dwell.

She closes her eyes, willing herself to calm

down. Think positive thoughts, she tells herself, but that doesn't help. Her eyes snap open. Glancing back at her is the Seifu look-alike, smirking at her, his tongue darting from between black lips like a serpent.

She turns away as a shiver runs the length of her spine. Suddenly, a barrage of images attacks her, bombarding her with a frightening intensity. She gasps for breath as she recalls Seifu and his torturous laugh. It's all coming back. Like a freight train, it barrels through her mind and she is powerless to stop it or throttle it back: the plane crash, Seifu, her mamma, Taj, the aftermath, the plane crash, Seifu, her mamma, Taj, the aftermath, the crash, Seifu, her mamma, Taj, the aftermath, the crash, Seifu, her mamma, Taj, the aftermath, Seifu, her mamma, Taj, the aftermath, Seifu, her mamma, Taj, the aftermath, her mamma, Taj, the aftermath, her mamma, Taj, the aftermath, Taj, the aftermath, Taj, the aftermath, the aftermath, the aftermath . . .

Cheyenne lets out a wail, loud and high-pitched. Half of the passengers snap their heads around searching for the origin. She begins to thrash about and scream, flogging the seat in front of her as if she were warding off a swarm of attacking insects.

The flight attendant is there in an instant, hovering over her with a fresh glass of water and a moist towel to comfort her, to no avail.

By the time they finally sedate her, Cheyenne is too far gone to care.

The belly of the jet glides over land, "feet dry," as it is sometimes called—and the verdant top cover of a tropical forest replaces the rush of emerald green waters. The irregular spikes of mountaintops soon supplant the gentle roll of hills. Dirt-filled or in-need-of-repair roads sprinkle the landscape; half-built houses dot the countryside—cement multistory carcasses with rebar ends protruding from the unfinished structures like punk hair. A goat, a pair of sheep, and a herd of cattle take up various spans of roadways—causing an all-too-familiar gridlock to which the natives have grown accustomed.

Taj's face is pressed against the glass, the glare from a brilliant sun searing his eyesight. He squints but does not want to miss a single detail. To be able to see the countryside in this raw splendor—from way on high—and to experience what he has dreamed for so long is a wonder he has trouble comprehending.

Indeed, it has been a long time.

Twenty years.

Suddenly, Taj is frightened. He senses that they are flying over the very spot where the Beech King Air fell from the sky on that fateful afternoon two decades ago, changing his life immeasurably. But he can't be sure. The mountains and surrounding landscape look quite the same.

Just then the pilot comes over the intercom, and in his thick, soothing Jamaican accent informs the passengers that they will be landing soon. Taj feels the plane decelerate and begin to lose altitude. But he is no longer afraid. He is going to make it.

A feeling of revelation is buzzing inside of him. He is elated and for the first time in days Taj feels *peace*. A quiet calm overtakes him as he begins to breathe slowly, deepening his intake, and cuts a glance out the window. Yes, they are still flying, still descending *normally*. The way they should be, all systems normal, the urban sprawl of Kingston in sight—soon now, just a few more minutes before they touch down onto the slick tarmac.

And Taj does something he has not done for twenty years. He thanks his God—the one to whom he hasn't spoken in a long, long time, and asks for His forgiveness.

The tarmac sizzles, just as he recalls from his nightmares. And Taj fights the instinct to bend down and kiss it. Instead, he slings his bag over his shoulder and walks merrily to the Norman Manley International terminal.

Inside, it is cool and very crowded. Passengers are being reunited with their loved ones. For a moment Taj has to move off to one side, put his bag down by a pillar, and collect himself. His thoughts return to his pop; he called him from BWI this morning and told his father of his plans. His pop listened attentively and didn't say anything until Taj was silent.

"It's what you must do, so go to it," his pop had said, wearily. "God will be with you."

"We shall see," was the only response Taj could muster.

He also thinks of Nicole—several days shy of Christmas—alone, perplexed, and full of anger. He should call her—tell her that he made it safe and sound, and that he loves her.

He vows to make the call once he is settled.

Taj moves to the line of waiting taxis— white mini-buses or vans that look to be about fifteen years old. He has made arrangements with the hotel, so a driver should be waiting. And indeed to the right stands a gaunt Jamaican holding a cardboard sign with his name. Taj huffs over to the car. He is already sweating although the temperature is quite comfortable.

The interior of the cab is hot. The windows are rolled up and the A/C is on high. Taj inquires if the driver can make it any cooler. The driver smiles, shrugs his shoulders, and says this is the best that he can do.

Although the ride should take no more than twenty minutes, it takes thrice that—for various reasons. There is traffic getting out of the city (there shouldn't be, but there is—primarily due to the condition of the roads), and Taj is dizzy getting used to riding on the left side. Throngs of dark men stand along the roadside offering up everything from warm sodas to DVDs to hats to smoked fish. They taunt the procession of cars, not satisfied with a "no, mon" from drivers or passengers. Taj's driver feels compelled to play tour guide, slowing down at every intersection and around every bend to point out various sights—some historical, most not.

"Over dere, mon, is where my grand-mom still lives," he says in a singsong patois. Taj is thinking that the last thing he wants to do is make small talk with this cab driver. It's not that he doesn't want to talk with the guy, but he's come all this way for a singular purpose and the nervous energy inside him is about to erupt. Taj wants to find his destination quickly, settle in, and make preparations for the next day. But then an interesting thing happens. Taj asks about a dilapidated old building on the outskirts of town that interests Taj from an architectural perspective. The driver seems to know a great deal about the building and its history. They settle into an easy dialogue, as if they have known each other for years but have been apart, and are using this time to catch up, like old friends.

The city gives way to thriving countryside and Taj is taken with the country. The natives spotted along the roadside are in no hurry, with a gentle gait that speaks to their rhythm and sense of time; the scrawny animals in seemingly peaceful coexistence with their masters. This quiet vision and the picturesque ocean that laps at delicate shores are incongruous with the harsh reality of poverty that floods the landscape.

Tiny, clapboard shops—one-room entities—are perched on the sides of the road marketing soft drinks and jerk chicken.

Outhouses are everywhere.

The conversation shifts. Why is Taj here? Vacation? Business?

Taj ponders the question, wondering how to answer it truthfully.

"Neither," Taj answers. "I am here because I am searching for something, a place that I visited in my youth. It is, I am sure, much different now than I remember, probably built up, paved over, or left to nature—overgrown and quite inaccessible. Regardless, I am here to find it."

The cab driver finds this response fascinating. He quickly offers to be Taj's guide.

"I know dees parts as well as de next mon—been here all my life," he says, flashing a smile as he eyes Taj through the mirror. Reggae is playing from the car radio—a monaural transmission, but both men are captivated and moved by the beat. "I got me dis car and it will go where you need it to."

Taj considers this as he is handed the driver's card. His cell phone number is scribbled underneath his name in black ink.

"It's in the mountains, this place is," Taj says, as if to warn him. "I'm sure we can't just drive straight there. It's going to take time and some off-roading to reach it." Taj suddenly has this vision of being in the Egyptian desert, searching for the hallowed tomb of some long-forgotten ruler as an unrelenting sun assails their ripening backs.

The cab driver's grin plucks him back to reality. "No problem, mon," he remarks excitedly. "My brudder? He got him a jeep!"

Fifteen

Taj, with terror and adrenaline mixing like a
Molotov cocktail as they coursed through his
veins, thought about what Pop would say if he chose
to turn his back on a fellow man. To do so is not
what the church or Pop had taught him. It was a
tug of war, a battle his brain was unaccustomed to
fighting. In the end, he braced himself against the V
of the dappled tree limbs, broke through the debris of
hydraulic lines, electrical cables, and composite ma-
terial to reach the rear of the cockpit. Seifu had been
hurt, but not badly enough that he could not move.
With Taj's help he was able to carefully extricate
himself from the hanging cocoon, and reach the
safety and sanctuary of the massive tree.

Taj had saved Seifu's life.

The past two hours had been a nightmare. Cheyenne sat on the ground, rocking back and forth,

staring off into space, calling out repeatedly for her mother. Her calls remained unrequited.

Cheyenne had begged Taj to leave Seifu. As soon as she heard his laughter, she had snapped out of her trance, ran to the base of the large tree, and screamed for Taj to leave him entombed forever. Taj could not. Extracting Seifu from the dangling no-secone, assisting him as he broke free from the chamber that bound him like a chick hatching from its shell was enervating—to the point that Taj could only collapse.

Please Lord, Taj prayed, please let me open my eyes and find all that I have witnessed turns out to be pure fancy. He waited an instant, thinking that God sometimes needed a moment to collect His thoughts before working His divine magic—but when he opened his eyes, what he saw electrified him.

Seifu stood before them, a look of insanity alighting from his bloody stare, leaning on his thick black cane, jeans ripped at the knees and stained with dark blood. Lacerations about the neck and face, eyes bloodshot yet alive with what could only be characterized as madness, he held a single, gleaming, razor-sharp blade between calloused fingers. A stream of unintelligible words spewed from his mouth like molten lava as his gaze swept between them and the shiny blade, a weapon that had been sheathed and sequestered in the small of his back, smuggled miraculously onto the plane before it crashed.

"Me de soldier 'mong us," Seifu commanded, pointing the walking stick at Taj and then to Cheyenne, "so me de master here. Yu listen tu me, we get out here den wun peece—don't listen? Well, den, we got problems." Seifu flashed a wicked smile.

"Just what have you done?" Cheyenne suddenly glanced up and yelled from her sitting position. "You made the plane crash—you're the one who is responsible. Where is my mother?!?"

Taj cringed as her voice elevated. He didn't trust Seifu as far as he could throw him. Guilt and doubt surged though his head. Had he done the right thing by helping Seifu? Had he, Taj, by rescuing Seifu, put his and Cheyenne's lives in further danger?

Seifu glared at Cheyenne, considered her words before spitting blood onto the ground by his feet.

"It no be me, chile—de damn pilot dere." He raised the blade up and pointed into the trees. "Me ask a simple ting—but he dere don't listen. Well, den, we got problems."

"Everything was going smoothly until you . . . and now my mother . . . what has happened to my mother? Where is she?" she yelled.

Taj stepped up, attempting to put something solid between the girl and Seifu. "What do you want? Why are we here? Why did you crash the plane? Please tell us?" Taj begged.

"*Me not crash de plane, yung brudder,*" he replied, calmly, but the sparks in his eyes were unmistakable. "*De pilot not take me where me need tu go. Dat's his fault—not me!*"

Taj spun around to take stock of his surroundings. He glanced at his watch and sighed—it was not yet noon. The temperature was bearable, since the sun didn't penetrate directly this far down to the forest floor. Shadows danced as the leaves and underbrush moved in the morning breeze.

"*Why, Seifu, just tell us why?*" Taj asked again.

Seifu's eyes seared into Taj. He was silent for a moment; his movements halted. He then reached into the pocket of his jacket and extracted a fat cigar. It was badly misshapen, so Seifu cleaved it in two, placed one half between his teeth, and sequestered the other away.

Seifu lit the cigar slowly, puffing on it with a concentration that frightened Taj—he then looked up.

"*Because of her!*" he yelled, pointing the knife at Cheyenne. "*Her, dere—she's da reason fer da strife. De world's not right 'cuz of dem womans!*"

It was late afternoon and hot. They congregated by the ruined cabin, moving away from the cockpit whose stench had wafted down and enveloped them. Taj was sitting in the shade of a tree—his shirt off, his taut back muscles covered with beads of sweat, *his light eyes blazing. Cheyenne was to his right several feet away. The two exchanged harried looks, but said nothing.*

Seifu paced a few yards away, the bandanna wrapped around his left elbow. He was shirtless and his dreads hung free. Taj watched him, scanned his fit body—dark ropy veins that fanned out across his well-muscled frame. Taj had no misgivings. He knew that he couldn't take him—the guy was trim and in excellent shape except for a limp and the bruises they all shared.

Most importantly, Seifu held the weapon.

Taj had gotten a good look at it. It was unlike any knife he had seen—and in his pop's line of work, he had seen more than a few. It was perhaps nine inches long and two inches at the widest point. It had dual edges, razor sharp, that led to a gleaming point. The handle was bone and shaped like a T, so that its possessor could grasp it by making a fist and have the blade point outward—an extension of one's fist. Seifu carried it in a dark leather sheath that was affixed to the inside of his jeans by the small of his back. He unsheathed it ceremoniously as if it were a samurai sword, and twirled it between his fingers and above his head, demonstrating to anyone within striking distance just who was the boss.

They had walked the area for a good hour until fatigue and hunger forced them back to base camp. They found wreckage: bits and pieces of the fallen airplane, sections of wing and fuselage, and bag-

*gage from their fateful trip, but no sign of the mid-
section that carried Cheyenne's mother. They had
collected what they could use and gone back to the
cabin where they sat, exhausted, hungry, and petrified.*

*Seifu paced about, rambling to himself, only to
bat at the air with his stick as he shook his head violently. The chubby cigar dangled from his teeth as
his dreads flung themselves at each other in a frenzied dance.*

*Cheyenne had taken her backpack and walked
away where under cover of a stand of palm trees she
changed into a pair of shorts. She returned, grateful for the air on her skin; her flowery shirt remained
on and stained with sweat. Her frizzy hair clung to
her scalp, and Cheyenne tried unsuccessfully to
comb it down with her hand every few minutes.*

*Taj watched her silently. She sat down on the
ground, her back resting against the base of a palm,
knees pulled to her chest, her bronze legs gleaming
in the sunshine as she nibbled on a piece of chocolate discovered in her knapsack. Taj followed her
contours with his eyes—she shined like a beacon.
Her skin was tight and smooth. She stood to stretch
and Taj sneaked a glance, mesmerized at that spot
where fabric met skin. He followed these lines too—
thighs to hips then navel to breasts—and the place
where her legs came together was dazzling like the
sirens, provocative, yet unfamiliar territory. Taj felt
the stirring of desire build within him. He tried to
tear his gaze away but found he lacked the strength*

to do so. He had never been this close to purity before.

Cheyenne—wedged in her own world and oblivious to Taj's stares—tapped her leg incessantly against a rock. He noticed that Seifu had ceased his pacing and was staring at her too—two men, very different—a wide chasm separating their characters, ages, origins, and beliefs, but bounded by common carnal desire.

Taj looked away, ashamed.

Seifu abruptly sat on the ground. He laid his walking stick out in front of him and closed his eyes, tilting his face to the sky. Taj stood up, frustrated and tired of feeling helpless.

"Seifu," he began, careful to keep the contempt from his voice, "this is crazy. We can't just sit here— we need to do something. We should move; for all we know a village could be fifteen minutes from here."

Seifu remained seated with his eyes closed. He pondered Taj's words before opening his eyes and settling his gaze on Taj.

"No, da one dey call 'Taj Mahal,' we stay here. The ting is, brudder," and he struggled to stand with the help of his cane, "no villagers come fer us—if dey wuld, dey be here now."

"Well, we need to do something. Her mother . . ." Taj gestured at Cheyenne, "is out there someplace— alive—and we need to find her."

Seifu closed his eyes again, glanced up, and shook his head slowly. As he opened his eyes, he panned from Taj to Cheyenne as he relit his cigar, and produced perfect O-rings of smoke that he sent onward toward heaven.

Cheyenne rushed to her feet.

"This is total . . ." she searched for the proper word, "bullshit, you hear me? My mamma is out there—she could be dead. I'm alone and scared. And you're crazy and can't help me or anyone else. I'm leaving!"

She reached for her pack, slung it over her shoulder, and glanced at Taj.

"You can do what you want, but I'm not staying here one more second. If I have to search for my mamma alone, I will. Anything beats sitting here starving to death!"

Taj felt his heart race. Cheyenne was right. They needed to do something. The problem was Seifu.

Like a cat he leapt up, extending his limbs as if there were springs attached, and sailed across the space in a manner that defied physical logic. Before Taj could react, Seifu had connected with Cheyenne, his thick, calloused hand across her back, knocking her to the ground. She yelped in pain as her palm rushed to cover the bruised skin. Seifu had her pinned to the dusty ground with his staff. She stared up, wide-eyed and terrified.

Taj moved without thinking. He lunged for Seifu, mindful that the knife was still sheathed and out of sight.

The staff came up, arced toward Taj's head, and connected with a sickening thwack! Taj fell like a rock, tasting blood between his lips. Before he came to rest on the ground, the staff was back in position, pinning Cheyenne to the ground.

Seifu's eyes blazed as he puffed on his cigar. "Yu tink yu can walk out?" he bellowed, bending down to stare at her. Spit flew from his mouth. Off to the side, bundled in a fetal position, Taj reeled from the pain. "No, pretty sista—me de soldier 'mong us. Yu just a flower!"

Seifu crouched down until he was inches from her face. He scanned her frightened features, then gazed down at her breasts and navel. His gaze dropped further to her shorts and tanned legs. He crab-walked back a foot, admiring her as he moved. Suddenly, he grabbed her ankle and yanked it up, and spread her legs wide. Before Cheyenne could react, he took the cigar in his other hand and branded her on the inner thigh—pressing the smoldering cigar into her flesh, searing her, baking her, burning her with his mark—a symbol of his power, forever.

Cheyenne screamed and thrashed about like a junkie in a straightjacket. She finally succeeded in throwing Seifu off of her.

It didn't matter.

It was too late.

The damage was already done.

Sixteen

There is something so serene and peaceful about sunsets. The way the light falters before your eyes, the sky changing in hue from profound blue to sunburst orange to indigo. And as the setting sun dips below the distant horizon, fading beneath the waves, it's as if one is saying farewell to a loved one or experiencing death by slipping into a watery grave—a passing of sorts, only to reemerge the following morning, brilliant, fresh, and anew.

Taj stands by the water's edge as he watches the fading sun. His toes are caressed by gentle waves that lap sensuously at his feet. He is alone as the sand turns cold on his skin. He watches the sun dip below the swells and stands for a long time with his hands clasped behind him, the moderate breeze caressing his dark neck, shoulders, and back.

Tomorrow it begins.

And he smiles—because he knows that in an instant, things can happen and change one's life forever. It did to him.

He was heading in one direction, like a ship bound for a distant country, only to be turned around, midway, because of *her*. She came back into his life, flinging open the doorway to a soul that had been quieted for so long. It took him back to the days of his youth and that extraordinary time that changed him forever.

Taj is not sad that he found her again. He makes no excuses for the way things have turned or for the way he feels now. He won't. That's the way life is.

Taj turns and makes his way back to the road and into a small, dimly lit bar with lazily turning ceiling fans and warped hardwood floors. He takes a table by the window so that he can watch the ocean's surge. He orders a shot of Appleton Estate Jamaican rum and chases it with a cold Red Stripe. Taj is not a big drinker, but tonight he needs the liquor to warm his insides and calm his nerves. The waiter comes and Taj orders the red snapper for supper.

He removes a topographical map from his knapsack and carefully unfolds it on the table. He glances at the map, something he ordered online. It is detailed enough for what he is planning to do. He thinks of the conversation he had earlier with Frankie the cab driver. He told the man to meet him tomorrow morning precisely at seven a.m. in front of the hotel, and to be driving his brother's jeep. Taj prepared him to be away for the entire day.

On the map there are various markings in felt pen. An area circled, roads highlighted, streams marked. Taj knows the general area where the plane went down or, more accurately, where they found sanctuary. He suddenly recalls that day as though it were last week, as well as the beefy Jamaican man in his impeccably pressed uniform with brass buttons that shone so brightly that Taj had to shield his eyes. Taj never found out which service he represented; at that point it didn't matter, but after all these years, he remembers with a mystical clarity the features of the officer who interrogated them—his thick imposing lips, skin as black as midnight, and closely cropped hair. That was the day that Taj and Cheyenne came out of the woods, worn down and near death.

That day they found refuge.

Their sanctuary. A calm after the storm.

That place has been circled on the map in red.

Taj stares at it forlornly as his snapper arrives. The scent of spices and wild rice wafts over him.

A place to begin. Tomorrow they will commence their search from there.

At the exact moment that Taj takes his first bite of snapper, savoring the flavor as he washes it down with a swig of ice-cold Red Stripe and stares out the picturesque window, about forty miles north of him stands Cheyenne, fully recovered from the ordeal on the plane, facing into the ocean's breeze. Her hair and body are scrubbed clean with strawberry-scented soap and a colorful blue-green sarong (handmade by Jamaican natives) is wrapped around her waist, accompanied by a matching top. She stands on the shore of Ocho Rios, the huge renovated Jamaican Grande towering behind her, which is a popular tourist attraction and a bus ride of several hours from Montego Bay.

Her feet, too, are dipped in the warm water that laps ceaselessly at her toes. Dozens of vacationers stroll past her, some lovers hand-in-hand. For a moment she thinks of Malcolm, and the pang in her chest tells how much she misses him.

A bony Jamaican in a Bob Marley hat comes up behind her holding necklaces in one hand and bracelets in the other.

"Some-ting for de misses?" he asks. Cheyenne turns politely and obliges him by perusing his collection. She selects a beaded necklace—alternating translucent stones of various pastels—blue, green, lavender, and pink. It reminds her of a building she saw on her way to the hotel, passing it as she rounded a corner of some nameless, poverty-stricken village. It was a simple structure that stood alone, deteriorating and badly in need of repair, but beautiful with the aquamarine sea as its backdrop—the top section painted a sapphire blue, the bottom a rich violet, and to the right, a shorter section was painted pink. Cheyenne had marveled at the structure, the lovely colors that together blended to create a postcard of art, and she wished that she had been quick with her iPhone to capture that tranquil scene.

"How much?" Cheyenne asks, holding up the necklace between thin fingers.

The man grins. "For you, pretty lady? Ten dollars!"

Cheyenne blinks then gives him the money. She places it around her neck and satisfied, continues down the beach.

There are a number of Jamaicans setting up shop directly on the sand. They are selling stuff that tourists will purchase by the tons to personally memorialize their vacations: large and small carvings, jewelry, artwork (some very elaborate), cheap trinkets, and other useless junk. As Cheyenne walks by, they call her over to check out their merchandise. She is polite, smiling as she moves on.

She is thinking about this trip. Finally she is here—after all of these years—time has whooshed by because she buried the memories deep in her mind. But now she is back. She has done the unthinkable.

Cheyenne has no game plan. Unlike Taj who, unbeknownst to her, is at the opposite end of the island, she hasn't come here for a specific purpose. She has no agenda, although there is a vein of an idea that is still percolating, forming in her mind's eye. She has glimpsed wisps of it, but they are fleeting and haunting to her. So, for now, she is going to enjoy her freedom: the feel of the warm sand on her skin, the light breeze that caresses her hair, the native rhythmic sounds that waft down to the water's edge, the food (her stomach has begun to grumble), and a quiet, cozy bed.

Tomorrow, after she is well rested and refreshed, she will decide if a plan is necessary or even desirable. For now, there is no need to rush.

Around midnight is when Taj awakens. He has been sleeping quite peacefully; the room is silent save for the soft whirling of air conditioning. Taj hears the tranquil sound of rain, soft at first then rising to a crescendo as thick drops slap against plump leaves. He lights a candle, then goes to the windows that face the ocean and flings them open. A fair wind is blowing and the palms surrounding the exterior of his room are dancing to the breeze. Taj watches the rain from the comfort of his room, the windowsill cool to the touch as he leans forward to let the breeze bathe his face.

The wind dies. The rain remains, a steady patter that is soothing and refreshing. Taj can taste it. The freshness hovers in the air.

It is after midnight and her room is black, but Cheyenne is wide-awake. Her room, like Taj's, is silent. She has shut off the air so that she can listen to the rain. The sliding door to the balcony is open, allowing her senses to be unobstructed. She sits fully nude directly in front of the open door, face in hands, toes pressed into the carpet (heels up, like a dancer). A thin layer of sweat adorns her bare skin giving her an appealing sheen. The rain is falling vertically; there is no wind to cause raindrops to collide. Across the expanse she can hear the rumble and growl of the ocean as tumultuous waves crash against the shoreline. These distinct sounds of rain and ocean meld to create a symphony that moves her to tears.

Like Taj—she is remembering that day.

She recalls a rainstorm similar to this one—
a long time ago when their fate was yet unknown. They had been pushed to the limit,
worn down by a crazed man, acute hunger,
and the elements—the hot, relentless sun
that beat down every day, and the sudden
rains that could soak to the bone.

A steady rain fell, the cadence of raindrop chatter
hypnotic; uncanny shadows moved to a ballet or-
chestrated by the storm. They had sought shelter in
the wrecked cabin, their sleeping nest and refuge
from the darkness and elements. But when they
heard the rain, they ventured outside.

Cheyenne first—slowly, because of her wounds
and fatigue that clung to her like a constricting
hug. She was cautious, as if something or someone
might be waiting for her out among the shadows.
But she swallowed what little fear she had left—at
this point most of her actions were autonomous—
and stepped into the driving rain.

She was soaked in minutes. As Taj watched from
the shelter of the derelict cabin, Cheyenne tipped her
head back and allowed the water to pelt her face
and neck. The feeling was therapeutic and she
drank it all in, allowing the power of the rain to
massage and heal until her muscles were once
again pliable.

She had moved off into the distance, away from
Taj and the damned cabin, toward a clearing where
even in this steady rain one could see details. She

knew Taj was staring at her. And she had no doubt that he was moved.

When she reached the clearing she paused, spent a moment feeling the fabric of her soaked clothes. Methodically she removed them—without fanfare—first her top that was grungy and torn, then her tattered jeans, finally her bra and panties. She left them in a heap by her feet and stood tall, her back to Taj and the cabin. Fully nude, she allowed the rain to cleanse her, infuse her with only what was good, and rejuvenate her spirit and mind—wash away the remnants of everything that was bad.

Taj recalls watching her, the desire he felt that night stirring inside of him like a hornet's nest. The way she moved with such grace and litheness, almost catlike; her form exquisite, inspiring, breathtaking . . .

Taj followed her with his eyes, his gaze never faltering or leaving her side. He was seeing a woman for the first time in all of her splendor—not a grainy photograph from some men's magazine his friend had found under his father's mattress, but a real, live-blooded woman.

Cheyenne's breasts were firm and upturned; her nipples were emergent like a flower to the sun's radiance. Taj watched her in profile and his breath caught in his throat.

As she turned her back to him, the fullness of her spoke to him. The curves of her waist, her long golden legs were magical. And when she pivoted like a ballerina and turned to face him, he saw the patch that covered her sex. Taj was overwhelmed with unfamiliar, intense sensations.

Taj ached for her—wanted her more than anything in his life. He longed to go to her, take her hand, lay her down on the softness of dark, moist Jamaican soil, lie down alongside of her, and devour those luscious lips. He craved to explore her body with the kind of passion reserved for soul mates and first-time lovers, a yearning more than the pangs of hunger that nagged at him constantly. He wanted to know her, memorize her features, imprint and emblazon the sights, sounds, touches, tastes, smells, and emotions of this day in his mind, so that he could return to this place, over and over, whenever he chose.

As he watched from the confines of the downed Beech King Air, he thought that he had never seen anyone as magnificent as Cheyenne, and he doubted that he would ever be blessed to see something this delightful and miraculous again. He was experiencing an orchestration of feelings and emotions that rose in pitch until his entire being was singing. The experiences of love and passion ignited inside him, leaving Taj forever changed.

He thought about following her into the clearing that day. Taj bit his lip until he tasted blood as he pondered his situation. He stood, exited what remained of the Beech King Air, and stretched as his head cleared the top, unsure of what to do next.

AWAKENING

Cheyenne turned the instant that Taj exited the cabin to feel what she was experiencing: the pounding, revitalizing rain on his skin. She was facing him now, hands at her sides, her long bronze hair dripping and hanging straight down her back.

With his own clothes soaked, his thick hair dripping as he eyed her jealously, he held onto the bark of a palm tree for fear of passing out. Inexperience paralyzed him and held him steadfast. In the end Taj could only watch his angel from afar . . .

Cheyenne is massaging her neck, reminiscent of the rains that had relieved her aches. Her hair hangs free, and as her fingers glide among the thick, strawberry-scented strands, she thinks that it is *his* fingers that touch her now, tugging gently, stimulating her scalp. Her hands move downward to her full breasts, where they pause on the rising ridges of areolas, circling them like honeybees, lightly pressing against both nipples in synchronous motion.

She remembers Taj and how his eyes followed her across the clearing; she could *feel* the weight of his stare on her. And despite the blaze that had sparked and smoldered between them, Cheyenne knows how that day ended.

Cheyenne closes her eyes, allows her fingers to snake down her torso to her navel, playfully probing the hole before moving on down toward her waiting sex, and re-creates the final scene between her and Taj—the way she wished that it had ended:

Taj reaching for her—his touch sending a quiver through her body like that of a tidal wave—caressing her arms, legs, back, and stomach with a light touch, feeling her cry out silently for him—opening her wings, inviting him in, out of the relentless rain, to a place that is warm and cozy.

She finds her opening easily and allows a finger to slip inside effortlessly. Cheyenne sucks in a breath and throws her head back as another finger finds its way inside toward her molten core. Cheyenne is moaning, her fingers are thrusting, and the rain continues its song.

She imagines him inside of her, his nectar-filled kisses and strong, lithe flesh pressing her into the muddy earth as he pummels against her, the yin and yang of loving—soft and hard, fast and slow, in and out.

She increases the drive, plunging her hand into her well with frenzied abandonment. Soon she cries out in song.

Cheyenne is thinking of Taj.

Taj is thinking of her.

The rain binds them, connecting them in the way an umbilical cord unites mother and unborn child. As the rain sprinkles the landscape, Cheyenne and Taj are far closer tonight than either of them knows.

* * *

Taj leans back into his window and sighs. The rain songs slowly fade, fanning out into the ethers and dissipating into thin air.

He reaches for his cell phone, powers it on and dials the number he knows by heart. It is late, but he wants, he needs to hear her voice.

After four rings, Nicole is not answering. Taj is forced to leave a message.

"Baby, it's me. I arrived safely and am well. I know it's late but I needed to tell you that I am thinking of you. I wish you were here with me so that I could share this lovely rain with you. Nikki, I hope you can forgive me for not being there with you. I do love you."

Taj powers down the cell and puts it on the bed. He extinguishes the candle as he blows on it gently.

"I love you too, Jazz," he says to the open window, hoping the sound will be carried on wafts of warm midnight air, which will transport this message to her, wherever she may be.

Forty miles to the north, the rain has ground to a halt. Cheyenne, invigorated yet exhausted, lies on the comforter, her still-sticky fingers tracing circles around the tattoo adorning her inner thigh.

She begins to hum the first few bars of "Love Me Still" from Chaka Khan, then sings a cappella to the quiet room, which is opened to the elements. She hopes the sweet words and her voice will rise up, escape the confines of this manmade structure, ride the updrafts of warm air, and carry her sound and message to Taj, wherever he may lay his head tonight.

Seventeen

*T*here was humming coming from beyond the clearing, but it was not Cheyenne. She lay crumpled by the base of a palm tree with thick bark that grows in sections to the top of the forest canopy. Cheyenne was in a state of delirium: her mother had been snatched from her grasp like coins from a child's hand, and her thigh had been seared and burned by a wild man. A few yards away, Taj lay on the cool ground, his body twisted as if he were the carcass of some half-eaten animal left to rot. Congealed dark blood covered the wound on his temple. The side of his head was misshapen, the swelling from the beating now the size of a seasoned lemon. Taj's eyes alternated between open and closed, staring upwards to the heavens, hoping and praying for a miracle—that someone or something would swoop down and rescue them from the madman named Seifu.

It had been this way for the past three hours—Seifu off in the underbrush doing God knows what while Taj and Cheyenne were left behind to tend to their wounds—the earlier lessons deep-seated and not easily forgotten. Seifu was in charge; he was their captor and would determine their fate. When they ate, drank, or moved on was entirely up to him.

Cheyenne's leg throbbed. She tried to hold it, but even touching her knee caused a great deal of pain. In the end, she couldn't do much except cover it with the juice from some fleshy leaves that Taj squeezed onto her burned skin. Cheyenne, in turn, had tended to Taj as best as she could, wiping the blood away with the bottom of her shirt and placing some cool leaves on his temple to soothe the throbbing pain.

They spoke little to each other; any communication between them would further incite the already crazed Seifu. Other than exchanging distraught looks, they were silent.

Seifu emerged from the trees holding a pile of kindling. He dropped it into a heap in the center of the clearing and ceased his hum. Taj noticed that his black walking stick leaned against the rear of the cabin by the plane's stabilizer. It taunted him, yet Taj was in no position to reach for it, let alone use it. Seifu knew this.

"Yu tu need tu gadder up—gonna be dark soon. Gonna need tu make de fire and find some ting tu eat."

Taj sat up, holding his head with his hand. Chey-

enne slithered upright, keeping her back to the tree as she eyed him silently.

"Ay, look dere at my flower, Norie, under de shade of de palm," Seifu said, tilting his head back to laugh. "It be tu hot fer yu dere?"

Cheyenne and Taj exchanged concerned looks. Had they heard Seifu right?

Seifu went to her and bent down, extending his hand to Cheyenne. She recoiled as though his touch were laced with poison. Seifu cocked his head to the side and gave her a fretful look.

"Are yu right, Norie? Not like yu tu pull away." He reached for her again. Cheyenne turned her face to the tree as Seifu's touch connected, his finger tracing a figure-eight pattern on her cheek. His voice had changed—it had warmed and decreased a notch, which frightened Cheyenne even more. This sudden transformation in temperament could mean anything.

"Please . . . ." she implored, tears seeping from her eyes and flowing down her face, "don't hurt me anymore."

Seifu pulled back and gave her a perplexed look.

"Why yu cry, Norie? Yu know dis man luv yu," Seifu said, clutching at his heart with a calloused hand. His gaze swept from Cheyenne to Taj.

Taj observed the exchange from his vantage point, with one knee pressed into the dusty earth. He glanced at the walking stick—so close—only twenty to thirty feet, max. Just a few short strides, he thought. But what would he do when he reached it?

Grab it and use it to bash in Seifu's skull? And what of Cheyenne? She was too close to that madman . . . in the time that it took for Taj to reach the stick, Seifu would be all over her, his gleaming knife at her throat. No, now was not the time to strike. Another time would come.

"Please," Cheyenne whimpered again, drawing backward into the shelter of the tree.

Seifu dropped both hands to his side and stood up. He backed away silently, shaking his head. Then a peculiar thing happened. Seifu began to cry. His cheeks were wet as the tears streamed down his face. His shoulders heaved and his body shook.

"Me not believe dis," he said, in between sobs. "Norie, Norie! Yu know me luv yu!" His sobs were heavy. Cheyenne and Taj could only watch in awed silence.

Suddenly, he went to her, knelt down, and placed his large arms around her shoulders, pulling her into him. Cheyenne squirmed, but was no match for Seifu. His sobs echoed throughout the clearing.

"Stop," she pleaded, attempting to push him off of her, "you're hurting me!" With a final thrust of Cheyenne's clenched fists, Seifu retreated backwards. He wiped at his eyes and watched her, reaching for her face. She pulled away.

"Me no understand yu, Norie. Me be good tu yu, give yu roof over yer head, and plenty food fer de belly. Me give yu luv, but dat ain't enough." Seifu stood and paced about the clearing, his voice beginning to rise in intensity.

"Dat's de problem wiv dem womans—never enuf. Me tink yu different, Norie, but me wrong!" Seifu remarked, his head shaking forlornly.

"Where wer yu before, Norie? 'Member yur gran fadder's farms in Haiti where life dere be hard—no play, no rest, nofing? 'Member, my flower? Dere be times wen yu tank me fer de rescue—so yu no work de farms no more. 'Member dat, Norie? 'Member yu so happy yu not go back tu de farms yu cry wid joy?"

Seifu increased his pacing, spitting his words at Cheyenne as if they were hot molten bits that singed his lips.

He stopped abruptly in front of her. *"'Member?"* he bellowed.

"Hey, Seifu," Taj said, rising from the ground. He swayed uneasily, and one eye—closest to his bruised temple—was pressed closed. But he managed to keep his open eye locked on Seifu. "Leave her alone—she hasn't done anything to you." Taj opened his hands and showed them to Seifu, so that there would be no mistaking his intentions. Taj was in no position to take on Seifu—that was certain.

Seifu cut a glance toward Taj.

"Lern frum me, yung brudder," Seifu said, pointing at Taj, *"womens, dey confused! Dey say wun ting, wen dey need yu fer a roof over der head and food in der bellies, but wen dey full dey forget who put dem dere!"*

He spat on the ground as he eyed Cheyenne. Seifu stood there for a moment, as if in deep thought, try-

ing to decide what to do next. Then he spun around and walked to the cabin, grabbing his cane before ducking inside.

They had hiked for a good couple of hours, Seifu using the distant mountain peaks as navigational aids as they made increasingly wide circles around the clearing where the Beech King Air had come to rest. After an hour of Seifu urging them on, they came upon a river that meandered about like a disturbed serpent. It was no more than thirty feet across, but the water was cold, fresh, and very clear. They stopped to rest. Cheyenne proceeded to soak her thigh in the water, lying down along the bank, oblivious to Seifu and Taj—just glad to have something cold and soothing on her burnt skin. Taj waded into the stream and dipped his head into the water, recoiling at the pain and the cold. But it was soothing, and he knew it was good for his wound to be cleansed. Seifu watched them from the bank, taking refuge in the V of a squat tree whose limbs leaned over the moving water. Other than splashing his face and taking a lengthy sip, Seifu remained in the tree, ever watchful of Cheyenne and Taj.

Taj made his way over to Cheyenne who lay in the water with her eyes closed, head tilted back, and hair swirling about.

"Are you doing okay?" he said, out of earshot from Seifu.

"Yeah, I'm making it," she replied. "You?"

"I'll live," he said. "Let me look at your leg." Taj bent down to examine her. She held out her leg for him, and he grasped her ankle gingerly. The river current flowed over her flesh, but Taj could see beneath the surface the damage that Seifu had inflicted. He looked closer. The burn was grotesque, the skin mottled and blistered, and Taj could see that the outer edges were blackened. He winced silently. He could feel her pain.

"This is the first time that it has stopped throbbing for a second. This cold water feels good. Do you think he'll let us stay here?" she asked.

"Doubtful—who knows what he's up to? Stay in as long as he allows; it will help bring down the swelling."

Taj wanted to run his fingers over the skin to soothe her, but he knew his action would have the opposite effect.

Cheyenne lowered her voice. "If I could reach that knife of his . . ."

"I know," he whispered to her. "I'm sorry I didn't do more to stop him," he said.

"Not your fault—the guy's crazy—he would have killed you if you had."

They both were silent as they processed that sobering thought.

"Thanks anyway," she said, and smiled weakly.

Taj looked at her. "Cheyenne—listen to me—we are going to make it. I don't know how, but we need to have faith and rely on each other. Together we'll figure a way out of this mess."

"*I don't know. Right now I'm having trouble finding my faith,*" she said. "*I don't even know if my mamma . . .*" She stopped because the tears had begun to flow. She reached over to splash some water on her face, wiping away the tears quickly.

"*I know,*" Taj said, "*but you can't give up hope. I have to believe she's still out there—and we'll find her. Soon.*"

"*I don't know . . .*"

Taj reached for her and touched her shoulder.

"*Have faith,*" he repeated. Cheyenne nodded silently.

Taj sat down in the water a few feet away. They glanced across to the riverbank on the other side. A hill rolled gently away toward a mountain ridge. He could see wild goats foraging in the pasture and felt a sudden pang of hunger. They would need to find food soon.

The scene was picturesque—rising peaks in the background, a rushing river in foreground, gentle hills populated with wild animals. If it weren't for a plane crash caused by a crazy man bent on violence, it would be quite serene and peaceful.

Cheyenne's hushed voice broke the silence.

"*That fucker has ruined me,*" Cheyenne hissed, "*My leg will never be the same.*" She had a look of melancholy on her face, as if she had accepted her fate, recognizing how powerless she was to change it.

Taj shook his head.

"*No, Cheyenne,*" he said. "*He has not ruined you or your spirit. He burned you, yes, and for that*

God will have His revenge, but do not for one second let him win," Taj pleaded. "You are not ruined. You will heal. And you will walk away from this a stronger person, you'll see."

The shake of her head told Taj that she was not in agreement.

"Look at my leg. Look at it," she said, raising it above the current. Water drops gleaned off her skin, and Taj glanced at the wound, which was reddened, raw, and blistery.

"Yes, I see it, Cheyenne, and do you know what I see?" he asked. She stared at him silently, waiting for him to continue.

"I see a flower—and a beautiful one at that. Are you familiar with jasmine, the fragrant flower?"

Cheyenne shook her head.

"See this pattern? It's difficult to discern now, but once the swelling and redness go away, it will be clear—like the petals of jasmine," he said, tracing the outline of the flower above her thigh as he spoke.

"It's called Jasminium," he said, "and it's one of the prettiest most, fragrant flowers I've seen."

"Jasminium," she repeated. "How do you know that?"

Taj smiled. "Introductory Botany. Junior year."

Cheyenne gave him the eye.

"What? A guy can't take a botany course?"

Cheyenne smiled.

"It's the Latin name for the genus or species of Jasmine. There are a number of varieties, but the one to which I'm referring has beautiful white flowers with petals that are shaped like that," he said, pointing to her thigh.

"I like that, Taj," she said, looking closely at her burn.

"You'll see. You will come to appreciate it not as a gross wound or burn, but as a beautiful thing—a flower that gives you character."

Taj stood, letting the water stream from his pants.

"Thank you," she said softly. "Thank you for that."

The flames crackled and sparked as they huddled around the makeshift fire. It was close to ten p.m. and the cold was descending upon them like the darkness.

Seifu had constructed the fire from the kindling he had collected. Thankfully, he carried a lighter. Taj couldn't imagine having to rub two sticks together to summon a flame with everything else going on.

Together they had found more water, following the river until it branched off and became a stream that meandered fairly close to their base camp. They had eaten, too. Seifu had directed them to collect as many freshwater snails as they could carry; he had used his bandana as a pouch. They had spent the early evening crushing the shells and extracting the meat—a time consuming and nasty task—especially for Cheyenne who was grossed out by the whole process. Afterwards, Seifu started the fire and found a piece of charred aluminum sheeting from the fuselage that he used as a pan. It took a while to cook the snail meat over the open flame, but in the end, he served them each a handful of fresh snails, considered a delicacy in certain parts of the world.

Cheyenne refused to eat, saying she'd rather starve to death than eat something that slimy. Taj had similar thoughts, but the hunger pangs were too intense to ignore. In the end, he swallowed them, shivering as they slid down his throat, grateful to have water to wash them down.

They were exhausted; the combination of wounds, work, hiking, searching, and heat made them extremely tired. Taj and Cheyenne used the sanctuary of the cabin to rest as Seifu kept a vigilant eye by the fire.

They could hear Seifu outside of the cabin, humming and speaking in his strange tongue—alternating between words that they could understand and others that were completely indecipherable. He spoke of hunting and his plan for capturing rabbits that intersected the clearing and ran through the underbrush. He mentioned that the river had to have fish, and that they should fashion a hook and line to catch them.

Taj and Cheyenne wondered why they weren't looking for signs of human activity. Surely a village or town was close by.

Cheyenne began to sing. It began softly as a hum after tiring of listening to Seifu and his ramblings.

Then, without music to guide her, she sang pure and beautifully as Taj watched silently. Cheyenne was not afraid to let him hear her voice, for by now, they had shared something deep and connecting— she felt comfortable sharing her talent with him.

Taj listened to her sing, thankful for her words and soothing melodies to remind him of things that were good. Soon, the ranting of a crazed man was long forgotten and they fell into blissful sleep, letting the darkness pull them down into the depths where there are no dreams, just sleep—untainted, profound slumber.

She felt his hot breath on her neck. She moved her head, turned away, but the hotness returned. She opened her eyes groggily and screamed.

Taj sat up with a jolt.

Seifu was crawling on top of Cheyenne.

"Get off of me," Cheyenne screamed.

Taj, without thinking pushed him off of her.

"What are you doing?" Taj yelled. "My God!"

Seifu was seething. Gone was the earlier consoling look. He leaned over her, the look of a madman in his eyes.

"So dis be how it tis, Norie!" Seifu bellowed, slurring his words as if he were drunk. "Now dat yu find some body else!"

In his hand he held a torch. The flames danced as his hand wavered, lighting the interior of the cabin. Taj could see that his eyes were red and blood-

shot. He appeared to have been crying. Cheyenne was balled up like a fist in the next seat.

"Yu bitch!" Seifu sneered as he grabbed at her leg. His fingernails made obscene marks as they slid down her calves. She kicked out, striking him in the chest. Seifu went backwards, the torch flipping in the air and showering the interior with sparks before smacking the seat cushion across the aisle.

Taj watched Seifu recover as he reached for the torch. He tried to grab the handle before the cushion caught fire. Putrid smoke began to fill the cabin. Seifu lunged at Cheyenne again, grabbing her ankle and twisting hard. She yelled as Taj grabbed onto her, trying to keep her from Seifu's grip.

They both were screaming. Seifu finally backed off as he suddenly noticed the fire that had started. He switched gears, frantically trying to fan the flames. He ran outside, grabbed a three-foot tree limb that lay on the ground nearby and beat the cushion until the fire was extinguished.

Cheyenne had scampered to the next row, attempting to put some distance between herself and Seifu.

Taj spoke first.

"Seifu—you almost killed us!" he yelled, oblivious to the fact that Seifu could reach over and strangle him with one hand.

Seifu's head twisted from left to right as he panted, the sweat popping from his forehead and running down his face. He ignored Taj. His gaze was locked on Cheyenne.

"Don't tink for wun minit dat me not know wat yu up tu. Me see wid dees eyes how yu look at dat West Indian boy—yu tink me stupid? Me see him comin' roun wen me be workin'!"

Seifu's chest heaved. He inched closer to Cheyenne, holding out a finger.

"Yu make baby wid dat West Indian boy—yu run 'way wid him!" He pointed his finger at his chest for a moment. *"Seifu see dis, Norie. And me knows wat tu du. Seifu take plane tu West Indies and find dem togedder."*

His eyes were blazing and Taj could feel the hotness of his breath as he spoke the words, words of pure molten hatred.

"Oh God," Cheyenne whispered, trembling in her seat.

Taj looked around frantically for something—anything that could be used as a weapon. He saw nothing suitable.

Seifu's face changed. Taj and Cheyenne watched the transformation: the softening of his lips, the tightness in his jaw that seemed to slacken before their eyes. He held out his hand, dropping the stick into the aisle.

"Come Norie—me have some ting fer yu. Wun last ting before yu go tu him."

Cheyenne was motionless—her eyes shifting rapidly from Seifu to Taj.

"Come," he said again, his words no longer slurred. *"Me take yu tu yer mudder."*

AWAKENING

* * *

"What did you say?" Cheyenne hissed. Her eyes were locked on Seifu. The fear that had been hovering over her moments ago was gone.

Seifu smiled as he backed up toward the cabin opening. His features were in shadows, his face haunting as he sneered.

"Norie—come tu me and me take yu tu yer mudder."

"WHERE IS SHE?!" Cheyenne yelled. "Where is my mamma?"

Seifu backed out completely. Cheyenne looked frantically at Taj who remained speechless.

She emerged from the cabin opening to find Seifu by the fire. He was sitting on the bare earth, staring at her silently. His walking stick was between his hands.

"Seifu—where is my mother? Take me to her now!"

"No, flower," he said softly, "Not yet . . ."

Seifu rose and went to her. He touched her chin delicately and she slapped his hand away.

"Take off yer clothes," Seifu commanded, his voice low but steady. He used the black stick to point to her shorts. Cheyenne blinked as she shuddered.

"What are . . . take me to my mamma!"

Seifu shook his head slowly. "Take off yer clothes and lie down fer me, Norie. Wun last time!"

Taj had emerged and was standing behind Cheyenne. He touched her shoulder and whispered for her to return to the cabin. She moved and Seifu saw that Taj now clutched the stick used to put out the cabin flames. He did not hold it in a threatening way, but his intentions were crystal clear.

"Leave her alone, Seifu," he snarled. "This has gone far enough. You will not touch her again."

Seifu pursed his lips as he rubbed both palms along the walking stick, staring at Taj before speaking.

"Young brudder—me not make trouble fer nobodies. But, she wants tu see her mudder, so she gonna take off her clothes and lie down fer me."

"No, Seifu, she is not,*" Taj said forcefully.*

"Yu tink dat stick makes yu a man?" he asked. "Yu tink dat stick gonna stop Seifu here? Me not tink so."

Slowly and carefully, Seifu reached behind him to unsheathe the knife. He extracted it, the blade gleaming in the semidarkness as firelight bounced off of its razor-sharp surface. He turned his gaze to Cheyenne who huddled behind Taj.

"Take dem off so me can see da nectar, my flower. Wun last time, Norie—or me cut yu, like de fish, me slice yu open from yer top to yer bottom, and den, yer guts will come out jus like dat!" he said as he gestured with his hands.

"Don't move!" Taj commanded, tightening his grip and raising the stick. "Don't you dare *move, Cheyenne!"*

Cheyenne stepped away from Taj—out of the shadows and into the clearing. She went toward Seifu.

AWAKENING

*By the fire, several feet from Seifu, she undid her shorts
and let them slide down to her ankles.*

*Taj stood motionless, his heart beating out of con-
trol.*

*Seifu motioned again with the stick. She slid down
her underpants.*

Taj closed his eyes and sighed heavily.

*Cheyenne lay down as Seifu watched without mak-
ing a sound. His tongue snaked from his lips before
he grinned triumphantly.*

*"Take me to my mamma, Seifu—that's all I ask,"
Cheyenne whispered.*

*Seifu did not respond. Instead, he used the black
walking stick to part her legs and insert the end into
her opening, his tongue dancing inside his mouth
as he watched her squirm.*

Eighteen

Taj walks the garden path that snakes to the ocean. Along the way he passes cottages and balconied hotel rooms whose inhabitants are, for the most part, still asleep. Fresh dew covers waxy leaves and closely manicured grass. The concrete path curves from left to right and back again, almost without rhyme or reason, but Taj does not mind. He is enjoying the stillness of the morning sun, the fresh oxygen that invades his nostrils, the many-colored birds that pierce the air with their trills and songs, and the full-grown iguanas that ascend the sides of lofty palm trees.

It is six forty-five a.m. Taj has already showered, dressed, and consumed a hearty breakfast comprised of a three-egg omelet, bacon and sausage, a helping of smoked whitefish, toast, and strong coffee. He normally doesn't eat excessively, but on this day he wants to be properly fueled. Today is not a day to skimp.

Taj sips at his coffee as he watches the sun rise into a brand-new sky. He is dressed comfortably—khaki shorts, lavender polo shirt, baseball cap, sunglasses, and hiking boots. The ocean is in front of him and a delightful breeze caresses his face. Behind him, he can see in the distance the mountains that rise up from the jungle as they attempt to touch the clouds, and Taj feels a twinge in his belly as he contemplates his day ahead.

He extracts a portable GPS unit from his knapsack, powers it on, and points it at the horizon. It takes a few minutes for the unit to find its position, receiving signals from a dozen satellites orbiting several miles overhead. The unit beeps, as if burping after a satisfying meal, announcing to Taj the precise latitude and longitude of his location down to meter accuracy.

He brought the GPS along to assist him in his search away from cellular coverage, but as he stares at the miniature LCD screen he finds it gratifying to know his position in this enormous universe. It makes him feel safe—as if he can't get lost again, not as long as he carries this device—with its invisible tentacles, a lifeline of sorts, which will ultimately guide him back home.

He is feeling good—very good—last night's

sleep was the best he's had in days—the deep slumber he fell into after the rain was peaceful and relaxing. He feels the vibration that buzzes inside of him. But it is a good sensation, nothing to be frightened or concerned about—this time, the shuddering within is a good thing.

It means Taj is ready to face his demons.

Frankie, his driver and guide, is parked on the circular red brick drive in the front of the hotel complex. The engine is running, A/C cranked, and Frankie, clad in nylon shorts and a Rolling Stones tank top, sits on the hood of his brother's jeep, taking a long, satisfying drag on a cigarette. He grins when he sees his fare, tossing his still-lit cigarette on the ground.

"We ready, boss?" Frankie inquires.

"We are," Taj says. And he is.

Taj removes the topo map from his knapsack and unfolds it on the hood of the jeep. He shows Frankie the area marked in red.

The place where they found refuge.

He shows Frankie the other landmarks that have been marked. But the red circle is their destination. Frankie nods and grins.

"No problem, mon," he says. "Every ting irie," he remarks as he lets in the clutch.

The drive takes them along the ocean, a curving two-lane road choked on either side with white gravel. Taj sees a number of native Jamaicans out and about: several women carrying baskets on top of their dark heads, a muscular middle-aged man, fully nude as he emerges from the waves and collapses onto the sand, still dripping from his morning bath. Animals litter the landscape. They pass sheep, goats, and cattle, and they are forced to stop several times because of the animals that lazily cross their path.

Taj is silent, drinking in the countryside like herbal tea, a satisfying, soothing chamomile that revitalizes his senses. Frankie, from time to time, chatters away about this thing or that, but for the most part, he keeps quiet, as if he can sense the change of mood in Taj—knowing that today is special—and is respectful of Taj's stillness.

The road changes—it is imperceptible at first, but Taj senses before he sees the change in grade—they are rising, into the mountains, away from the fresh morning sea breeze and toward the emerald hills that undulate like the wings of a sea ray. They are perhaps no more than thirty miles as the crow flies from *ground zero*—their destination; but with the winding, twisting roads that are in dire straits, it is anybody's guess how long it will take them to get there.

Taj pays attention to the surroundings. His face is pressed against the cool glass as he attempts to find patterns that are familiar to him.

Nothing yet. But they are getting close. Taj can feel it.

Thirty minutes into the drive, Frankie steers the jeep off of the blacktopped road and onto a narrow dirt track. He downshifts and revs the engine, spinning the back wheels in the dusty earth as the jeep pulls off to the edge. There are thick, looming trees everywhere, and it is cool here—the shadows from the dense canopy providing ample shade. Taj consults the map before reaching for the GPS unit; he presses it to the window and waits for it to calculate their position. It is then a simple matter of cross-referencing their position on the map.

Not long now. He feels the trembling mount.

Taj gets out to stretch and inhales a deep breath as Frankie draws on a cigarette. They make small talk. Frankie doesn't ask many questions. He has concluded that this journey is deeply personal for Taj and that Taj will let him in when he is ready. But not before. Frankie extinguishes the cigarette with the toe of his boot before they drive on.

Deeper and higher they go, following the winding dirt road as it meanders across the foothills of the mountains. Out here, the sky is completely clear and a pulsating cobalt blue. It strikes Taj that it almost appears airbrushed— as if it would be impossible for nature to create a sky with such a rich color. They pass very few houses—mostly single-story clapboard structures, seemingly haphazardly built. Short brick chimneys emit charcoal-gray smoke trails as fires are stoked for breakfast. They continue over wooden bridges built by hand and bubbling, frothing streams. Goats and sheep graze in the distant meadows. Taj is transported back to that time when he and Cheyenne lay down on a riverbank similar to the one they pass along now, the cool water lapping at their elbows as they soaked their wounds. Then, like now, the majestic peaks were in the distance, evocative of an exotic travel postcard.

The anxiety begins deep within his chest and stomach—similar to hunger pangs, except Taj is far from hungry. He feels the energy throttle up a notch and he glances around and behind him, taking in the contours of the earth, the shapes and patterns of the trees, the gentle roll of the hillside, the chatter of the streams. Taj knows with a sudden intensity that he is *close.*

He can feel it. The tension reverberates inside of him—a symphony of rhythmic chants—as the jeep presses on. Taj is not afraid.

A bend in the road up ahead grabs his attention. There is something poignant and familiar about this turn—the way the trees are placed on either side of the dirt road, their hanging branches sweeping the dusty ground when the wind blows—and Taj knows that he has seen this place before . . .

Taj sucks in a breath as they round the corner. And then he sees it.

A small church stands before them, constructed of red and brown bricks. There are about two-dozen wide steps that lead to thick wooden doors. The structure features a domed roof of smooth cement topped by a thin steeple, whose apex is capped by a lone bronze cross. It is a simple design, yet one that seems transplanted and out of place. Dual stained glass windows that depict the Virgin Mary and the crucifixion of Christ face the rising sun. Beneath the stained windows, a courtyard encloses a small cemetery to the right.

There are no vehicles or signs of any life anywhere.

Taj knows this place. As sure as there is a God, he has been here before.

Their sanctuary . . .

A calm after the storm . . .

"Good morning!" the waiter announces to Cheyenne who sits bright-eyed and awake. "May I pour you some fresh coffee?" he asks as he holds a cup and saucer between gloved fingers.

"You may," Cheyenne responds. She sits facing the ocean with a deliciously lovely breeze embracing her face and extremities.

Cheyenne feels wonderful. She stretches out like a cat after a long nap, and feels her blood pulse. She slept magnificently after the rain and that private sensual interlude that left her feeling energized and brand-new, ready to turn her face into the wind and accept whatever comes her way.

She sips at her coffee, her mind completely free and devoid of thought. She simply exists, observing the chaos of ocean swells, the emergence then retreat of wave after wave, eyeing a distant fishing vessel that bobs lazily along the still horizon.

Cheyenne is in no rush, possesses no attack plan or agenda today. No, today she simply is going to live—one glorious moment at a time— follow her footsteps and see where they lead her.

She orders breakfast, tempted by the variety on the menu, but in the end gives in to her craving for eggs over easy, fried potatoes, and toast. Cheyenne puts down her cup and stares across the sea. She lets thoughts of Taj permeate her psyche, arousing every inch of her lovely body until she sings.

Yes! Today is going to be a perfect day! Oh, to be sitting across from him right this moment, stroking his arm, laughing together . . .

Stop it, she tells herself. This line of thinking is not right.

But then with a quick shake of her head she tosses that thought away, and resumes her train of thought. This time she won't deny herself that which is long overdue.

Taj. Oh yes! Wouldn't it be wonderful if he were here? The two of them with flesh pressing together, interlocking like the fingers of lovers, lovemaking intense like the rains, their sweat and juices blending wherever they join. Afterwards, as they lay there, the afterglow of sex covering their bodies, limbs intertwined, they stroke each other softly, chests heaving as they smile and stare into each other's eyes.

Yes, it would be wonderful to see him again. If only for a moment more . . . to say the things that have been bottled up inside of her, held back, like hands that press on a gaping wound, trying in vain to contain the bleeding that oozes between fingers.

No—this is not right! She is a married woman who is in love with her husband. What does this say about her marriage and her vows?

Again, she shakes her head. Now is not the time to analyze or to consider these things. Cheyenne wants to open up and dream. Let these visions that are fluttering around inside her head float free—up and away, into the ethers, until she is unbound, no longer a slave, no longer held captive—at last allowed to *live* . . .

Cheyenne is not sad. She knows that she will never see him again. But it feels good to unleash and consider the things that she was afraid to imagine before. She smiles because she knows that her dreams are only good. And she is not bad or damaged because of her thoughts, no matter how impure some may consider them.

Her breakfast arrives and Cheyenne pauses to eat. Before she places the fork of hot runny yolk into her mouth she remembers that Taj was her last thought before falling asleep last night, and he was her first thought when she arose this morning.

Cheyenne will make no apologies for that.

Frankie kills the engine and exits the jeep with a flourish. Taj remains in the vehicle for a moment more, his gaze sweeping upward to the steeple and cross that, like a lighthouse, guide the uninitiated. There are so many thoughts and images flying through his mind at this moment that he feels dizzy—but he exits anyway, placing both feet on the ground and stepping away from the jeep to walk toward the stairs. Frankie observes him but does not follow.

Taj pauses, looks around, and seeing no

one else, continues up the stairs. He reaches the door and places a palm against the dark wood, feeling its smoothness, checking for a heartbeat. The cold brass handles are large enough for both hands to fit inside; as he pushes, the door groans and opens slowly. Taj goes inside.

The interior of the church is darkened. Sunlight from the rising sun assails the stained-glass windows, creating a kaleidoscope of colorful shades and patterns on the wooden floor and across rows of empty pews. Taj stops at the last pew and reaches out for support.

Suddenly he is feeling nauseous and afraid of passing out. It is coming back, full blast—all of it—and he isn't sure he can stand the force.

The hefty Jamaican policeman and medics rushed around Cheyenne as she lay on the make-shift stretcher with her blood slowly draining onto the cold wood floor. As she slipped away, down into the abyss to die, Taj clutched her hand. Outside in the narrow courtyard were two freshly dug graves.

Taj almost topples over with pain; the ache of remembering burns inside, but he is strong. He swallows the throbbing, acidic hurt that eats away at him and stands tall, exiting the church before he falls in too deep.

Frankie is taking a long drag from an unfiltered cigarette and staring at the distant mountains when he sees the wooden door open. Taj emerges.

"Let's go," Taj says to him. Frankie has time only to extinguish the cigarette before Taj vanishes to the left of the church and into the woods.

The GPS is his compass; the topo map his guide. Taj has a general idea of where he needs to go. The map has been extremely helpful in this regard—it pinpoints the location of the rivers and streams—and Taj has spent a great deal of time studying its details. He recalls how they came to the church (a hike of no more than several hours from the crash site) and remembers the general direction they had been moving—away from the setting sun whose ebbing rays made it impossible to recall the forest details. But Taj knows that he can get close—streams and other landmarks will get him there—and then with Frankie's help, they will hone in on the spot where twenty years ago a pair of young people were held captive against their will.

An hour into their hike Taj and Frankie cross a shallow stream. Taj pauses, places his knapsack on the ground and looks around. The terrain isn't familiar, but something tells him to follow the water downstream. So they do—for another twenty minutes, until fatigue has Taj stopping by a bend in the stream and a rocky outcrop of shale jutting out of the earth at a strange angle. He sits on the dark rocks, glances around, and checks the GPS and map to confirm their position. Frankie pulls out a canteen from his backpack and takes a swig.

Taj spins around wildly. Suddenly, he recognizes this place.

Yes. The trees are fuller, underbrush thicker, but the curve of the stream and rocky outcrop are the same when viewed from a different angle—Cheyenne and Taj made it to this spot once. The details of that encounter, however, elude him.

"We're close," Taj says to Frankie, who nods solemnly. For Frankie, this journey has become more than just another fare. He is glad that he was chosen to accompany Taj.

Taj wracks his brain—where in relation to this spot is the crash site? How far away are they? And in what direction? The answers are not forthcoming. He butts his forehead with his closed palm.

Think, Taj! What brought you here previously? Nothing. Trying to force it does *nothing*. He tries to make small talk with Frankie, but realizes that he is a ball of nerves—synapses are firing like a twelve-cylinder engine. He can't waste time shooting the breeze—not when they are this close.

Taj orders them to move on, away from the stream and deeper into the forest, following the contours of the land as it gradually slopes upward toward the distant peaks. The trees become thicker and the light more muted as they go deeper, shadows flickering at every turn. Frankie is silent, constantly gazing upward, as if at any moment something not of this earth will come sweeping down from tree-top level and devour them before either of them can react.

Animals flourish here—rabbit, wild boar and goat, deer; various kinds of tracks and animal droppings are noted. Different shades of exotic birds are spotted that on any other occasion Taj would stop to study.

But not today.

When they have been hiking for thirty minutes more they stop to rest. Both men are visibly tired. The exertion is taking its toll on them—Taj especially—while he is athletic and in good shape, hiking in Washington, D.C., is not a competitive sport. Plus the heat, however muted through the trees, is unremitting. Taj finds the foundation of a tree on which to rest and hydrate, while Frankie collapses on the ground in front of him. They remain there, not speaking for a good fifteen minutes.

Taj is having trouble getting a signal on the

GPS. Tree cover is in the way—so much for technology.

He stands, extending his arms outward while stretching his calves. He looks behind the large tree where he rested and spies a clearing to his right, beyond a stand of thick trees.

A clearing.

Fully nude, she allowed the rain to cleanse her, infuse her with only what was good, and rejuvenate her spirit and mind—wash away the remnants of everything that was bad.

Immediately Taj sprints toward the clearing, leaving the lounging Frankie behind him. "Hey, boss?" Frankie yells.

Taj stops in the center of the clearing and pivots on the balls of his feet. He glances back at Frankie. Taj grins and yells for him to come. By the time Frankie grabs the packs and hightails it to the center of the clearing, Taj has disappeared.

Frankie follows through another set of tall trees whose canopy dims the light. The forest ground here is quite damp and cool. He finds Taj standing in front of a large mound. It is covered with thick twisting vines, weed grass, and two decades of mud and dirt.

But the curved, off-white metal that peeks out from the edges of the thicket is unmistakable. Taj has found the derelict cabin.

Nineteen

Azure water licks at Cheyenne's toes and the feeling is highly sensual. Her sun-glass-covered eyes are shut; her hair hangs free, dipped in the water as foam-covered waves attempt to carry it out and back with the tide. She lies in a low beach chair clad in a bikini, one she picked up from the hotel shop—a nice colorful thing that barely covers her flesh—something she just *knows* Malcolm would not approve . . . but then again, Malcolm is not here!

The sun is a flaming orb directly overhead. She is painted in sunscreen, oiled up like a bodybuilder, and folks, both native and tourist, can't keep their eyes off of her lovely form.

Cheyenne smiles to the passersby who make eye contact and waves to children who play in the ocean. Several hundred yards out, folks on jet skis and kayaks playfully attack the waves. A handful of adolescents are snorkeling in the clear shallow water. The beach surprisingly is not crowded at all, and for the most part, she is alone—Cheyenne has a nice wide patch all to herself.

She turns over onto her stomach, giving her back to the sun. The bikini barely covers anything, but she doesn't care—Cheyenne's on vacation and will never see any of these people again. She reaches for her Toni Morrison book and selects a new playlist on her iPhone.

As she reads, Cheyenne sings to herself, accompanied by the music in her ear buds. Although no one comes close enough to hear, if they did they would marvel at the purity of her gift—a voice that sails, shimmers, and shines.

Cheyenne sings the blues. She sings of love, profound and pure, remarkably lost then found; of pain and sorrow; and of good times with friends, family, and children. Singing for her is therapy; it is expressive, energetic, sometimes explosive, but always cathartic. She finds that she can attack a problem with greater resolve once she's sung and liberated her spirit. Singing has been a source of stimulation and cleansing for her ever since she was young.

She gets up and removes her headphones, dips her ankles in the refreshing water to remove the clinging sand, then decides that every square inch of her pores is screaming to be licked by the sea. Cheyenne wades out waist high before diving under the waves, a smooth graceful move that leaves little wake topside. For a moment, she glides beneath the surface as she parts her hands, opening her eyes so that she can take in the totality of this underwater experience, swimming free past a bank of seaweed and kelp that tickle her breasts and belly as she swims by.

Surfacing, she explodes into the brilliant sunshine like a humpback whale, flipping her hair backward in an arc of water that sends droplets careening off her bronzed skin and into the ocean-scented air around her. Cheyenne exits the water slowly as people cease their activities to stare in awed silence—visions of a mermaid—water streaming down her tan body in rivers, thick hair winding down her back as she moves, hips swaying voluptuously, and smile breathtaking to behold. Onlookers follow her every move as she saunters over to an outdoor bar with a thatch-covered roof. She orders a frozen strawberry daiquiri from a grinning Jamaican lady and feels the energy course through her veins as the cold drink slides down her throat.

Music plays in the background—a thumping bass-infused groove from the band Third World. Cheyenne begins to sing along since she knows the words by heart; bar patrons pause in conversation to listen and stare. She begins to dance—her frozen strawberry drink in its plastic cup in one hand, extending her finger into the air with the other as she twirls around, delighting everyone around her. The entire bar is watching her. Cheyenne sings louder, becoming the spotlight for all eyes and ears. An elderly couple—an aging gentleman with a potbelly, chalky skin, and a cowboy hat sitting alongside his wife with lobster-red tan lines, coiffed hair, and gaudy jewelry—watches, amused. Cheyenne reaches out for the man's hand and pulls him to her as the bar begins to clap to the beat, and Cheyenne and Mr. Cowboy Hat spin around on the sand dunes while his wife cackles with glee.

More people join in, and before long, everyone is moving to the music and Cheyenne's vocals. When the song is over, she receives a peck on the cheek from the cowboy hat man and thunderous applause from everyone else, and executes a ballerina bow before heading back to her lounge chair, frozen drink in hand.

And then it hits her, square in the solar plexus—she has never sung in front of complete strangers like that before. It's amazing, but true. With the gift that she possesses, one would think Cheyenne would be on stage every chance possible. That's what Malcolm thought. But it's just the opposite with her.

AWAKENING

She is petrified of singing in front of people and has a terrible case of stage fright—to the point where she won't sing in public. Not ever.

This issue has been a constant source of tension and frustration between Cheyenne and her husband. Malcolm being the record company man who holds the reins could make her career *happen*. But she won't allow it. Because she knows that such a career would involve getting on stage or in front of a camera, which is unacceptable to her.

So then, what just happened a moment ago, she wonders? She went for it, and it felt wonderful. Cheyenne became so caught up in the moment, living in the instant as though nothing else mattered. She existed for the here and now, without thinking or analyzing why.

Cheyenne reaches her patch of sand and lies down. Farther down the beach is a couple walking hand in hand. As they near, Cheyenne notices that it is two women—mother and daughter. They are immersed in conversation as they swing their arms together, their feet slashing through the surf. And in that instant, suddenly everything good that she was feeling drains out of her and she is left with a gnawing, numbing sensation that makes her queasy.

Mother and daughter.
Her heart aches from remembering.
In a flash she is transported back to that
dreadful time and place.

*Seifu could not be trusted—he had lied to her,
and to add insult to injury he laughed about it.*

"Take me to my mamma—now!"

Seifu's only response was to laugh.

*As she lay there in the diminishing firelight, in
the aftermath of rape, wheezing and coughing as
she bled onto the dank ground, her heart hardened
into a diamond, and she resolved to kill the man
who had taken her innocence.*

*Taj stroked her face but glanced away, respectful
of her nakedness. Seifu made sure Taj didn't move,
but he could not make him watch. Taj was unable
to bear the sight of Cheyenne's torture. Taj knew
that having an audience would have been another
nail driven into her coffin.*

*When her chest quieted, she began to sing—softly
and peacefully, almost a whisper, but with a purity
that bore into Taj's soul. He held her hand and
draped a jacket over her shivering form. She lay on
her back with her eyes closed, as if that would hold
back the tears from sprouting. When she finished
her song, her eyes opened and the tears fell.*

*Taj ceased his stroking, bent down until only
inches separated them and whispered to her: "Jazz,
look into my eyes . . . focus only on my eyes . . ."*

194

AWAKENING

It was those eyes, Cheyenne recalls so vividly, that gave her strength and the sustenance she needed to live another day. His voice calmed her—helped her reach a place where she no longer felt chilled and consumed with unrest. Those beautifully consoling eyes helped her attain peace.

And for that she would always love him.

She hated Seifu with a passion that frightened her. He had violated her, not once, but in the subsequent days, repeatedly. He laughed when she spit in his face. She longed to die—exit this world rather than face another day of humiliation and pain. She eyed the blade that controlled her—got to know its contours as though it were a second skin. She dreamed of plunging the blade deep into Seifu's heart—no, Seifu didn't possess a heart. Rather his eye; stab him through those reddish orbs that burned with hatred until he ceased to see . . . and breathe. Cheyenne hated him more when she was Norie to him—the back and forth, in and out of his psychosis, leaving her dizzy and distrustful of every word he spoke.

Taj felt the same. He eyed Seifu with a hatred that was thick and putrid. He yelled at Seifu and demanded to be freed! Seifu only laughed louder.

Time had a funny way of twisting around on itself like a Möbius strip—until they had lost track of how long they had been held captive. Had it been a few days or a week? Taj and Cheyenne could no longer tell.

And that petrified them. They were slowly dying . . .

Taj knew that Cheyenne's mother was dead. She had to be; there was no way that she could survive this long on her own. But he kept his thoughts to himself. Cheyenne demanded to see her. In her mind, there still was a chance that her mamma was alive. But after a while, even Cheyenne's eyes began to dim. Mamma was gone; she knew it in her heart.

Why wasn't anyone searching for them? A plane had gone down—they had been expected. What of the church mission? Surely they would send out a search party?

But as time spun on, it became clear that help was not on the way. They were alone in some Third-World backcountry—or so it seemed. This was not America where technology tracked the movement of planes and the country's military personnel responded to civilian disasters.

Some days Cheyenne would be too weak to stand and Taj would get water for her to drink and food to sustain her. Seifu had caught a few rabbits and had cooked them on a makeshift spit; besides that they foraged for nuts and berries or bitter leaves.

Seifu would not sleep in the cabin with them for fear that they would attack while he slept. Instead, he sought refuge in the forest, away from the clearing. Where exactly Taj and Cheyenne never knew, but he was watching them, always close by, he warned, in case they tried to escape.

The bleeding had ceased, only to commence again

every time Seifu used his wretched stick. Cheyenne hated the sight of that thing—the tool that violated her and damaged her insides. At times she wished it were Seifu himself raping her instead of that damned stick, but Seifu couldn't or wouldn't do that to her.

Not to Norie.

At one point she drew her teeth back and screamed at Seifu. "Why don't you be a man and fuck me, you black bastard! Stop using a cane to do a man's job!"

Seifu kicked her in the face with his boot for that remark. Taj lunged at him, no longer caring if he lived or died. He was beaten for his efforts until he could hardly stand, Cheyenne screaming as she lay in a pool of her own blood.

The sky is clear and cloudless, the sun strong. The breeze and ocean spray are delightful, yet Cheyenne is crying now as she relives that horrible time.

Taj saved her again and again.

With his words.

With his valor.

With his soul.

"Jazz, look into my eyes . . . focus only on my eyes . . ."

Cheyenne wonders if he knows just how thankful she is.

It was time to lie down and die. Taj and Cheyenne, after repeatedly being humiliated, trauma-

Devon Scott

tized, brutalized, and beaten, reached this decision simultaneously but independently.

Seifu no longer talked lovingly of Norie, or of his affection for her. Hatred ruled the day, commanding his every action. Seifu was spiraling farther into madness, and both Taj and Cheyenne knew that they had little time left.

They were famished and weak to the point that hiking the fifteen minutes or so to the stream sapped their dwindling energy. On most days Cheyenne could sit or stand for no more than an hour, considering how much blood she had lost. Taj fed and bathed her as if she were a child, his child, *knowing with certainty that she would die if he ceased his actions or if anything were to happen to him.*

Seifu also knew this—and Taj wielded this power like a weapon.

It was his weapon.

It guaranteed his safety.

Cheyenne's eyes were glazed and fading. Taj leaned in toward her and whispered quietly, for Seifu, ever distrustful of their time alone, was right outside the cabin.

"Jazz—I can't take one more night of witnessing Seifu hurt you. I can't."

Cheyenne nodded silently and reached up to stroke his face.

"We have to do something. I'd rather die than live one more day like this." He paused, waiting to see her reaction. Cheyenne nodded again, urging him to continue.

"*I want to kill him so badly I can taste it; forgive me God for uttering these words.*"

"*I know,*" she said. "*I know.*"

"*I'm going to do it . . . or die trying, because I can't face another night of watching you suffer.*" Taj was crying softly, the tears streaming down his cheeks.

Cheyenne sat up. "*Taj, you have already saved my life. If it weren't for you,*" she whispered, leaning in close to him, "*I'd already be dead. I hoped and prayed my mother would be delivered to me, alive and unhurt, but that hasn't happened.*" Her eyes grew narrow and moist. "*I guess that's not in God's plan.*"

"*We can take him, Jazz, but I need you to help me. Together we can beat him down. But I need you to protect yourself—can you do that? If I give you a stick, can you do that?*" he asked her.

"*Yes, Taj, I can,*" Cheyenne whispered. "*And like you, I'm ready to go to my grave trying. I'm so tired.*"

Taj stared at Cheyenne long and hard—the glassy eyes were gone, replaced by cold resolve. And in that moment, he admired her more than anyone he had ever known, because she had endured a lifetime of pain and yet still possessed the strength to fight her enemy.

Cheyenne was one amazing person. One amazing girl.

Taj wiped away the tears and thought about his pop. He wondered if he would understand his decision, and hoped that he wouldn't hate him for what he was about to do.

"God forgive me," he whispered and said a silent prayer.

Cheyenne watched from the muted shadows of the cabin, no longer interested in prayer or rhetoric with God.

He had abandoned her.

He had abandoned them all.

Twenty

The feeling Taj has is indescribable. He stands before the damaged cabin whose exoskeleton has been covered over with vines, brush, and striations of mud. Decades of heavy precipitation and sun have dulled the metal fuselage: it is dirty and full of grime; mold spots adorn the exterior, and the glass portholes were shattered years ago. Yet the emotions that well up inside him and sprout forth are as fresh as the sun that paints his back and bald head with its radiance.

But the tears do not come. It is as if there are no more left. There simply is nothing left to give.

Frankie is silent. He is feeling as if he has entered a sacred place—a hallowed tomb undisturbed for generations. He clears his throat, mindful of the intrusion but unable to keep his curiosity to himself any longer. Frankie asks the one question he's been dying to ask all morning.

"What is this place?"

Taj turns slowly to face him.

"The remains of a plane that crashed twenty years ago," he says as he reaches through a labyrinth of leaves and thick vines to touch the dilapidated fuselage. Connecting with it, flesh to metal, opens the floodgate.

"I was on this plane," he says, morosely.

Frankie is silent. Words fail him—he doesn't know what to say.

Taj kneels on the ground as the distress in his body takes over. His eye begins to quiver uncontrollably. Aware that his mind and body seem to be operating without a captain at the helm, Taj does nothing to quell the vibration. It rips through his eyelid and cheek for nearly a minute. When it subsides, Taj slowly and carefully assesses the damage as one would after an earthquake. He gingerly touches his face and eye, but the tremor has vanished.

Kneeling before the cabin, Taj allows himself to remember everything; he's come too far to turn around and not face his worst fears. It happened on the very spot where he kneels. His gaze sweeps over the forest floor to the clearing behind them. So much happened in this tiny space—a prison without bars.

Everything had been bottled up and stored away, fermenting like an expensive wine. Now the images return—the details bitter yet clear. They run though his head, first at breathtaking speeds, and then at a reduced pace, throttled back. Taj has no choice but to relive the ordeal.

He turns to Frankie and asks in a low voice if he can have some time alone. His driver nods and backs away toward the clearing, noticing as he goes that Taj begins to shudder: his shoulders heave as he breaks down. Frankie wonders if he should go to him and provide comfort, but then thinks otherwise.

Frankie cannot do anything for Taj. Instead, he wonders what it must be like to be in a plane crash and *survive*. And he reasons how lucky Taj must be since he walked away.

Cheyenne waltzes into the lobby of the Jamaican Grande wearing a red and white sarong that covers her bikini bottoms. Her sunglasses are perched on top of her forehead. She has brushed her hair back into a ponytail. She heads for the lobby and asks to speak to the manager.

"Afternoon," she says with a bright smile, "I

need to speak with someone who is extremely familiar with the island. Someone who knows landmarks."

The hotel general manager, a youngish-looking Jamaican with closely cropped hair and a contagious smile, grins widely as he admires Cheyenne.

"Of course, madam. It would be my pleasure to assist you. What specifically do you need?" he asks in perfectly spoken English with just a trace of accent as he ushers Cheyenne to a seat in front of an ornate desk in a back office. The desk is spotless save for a rotary black phone and a legal pad. He takes his seat behind the desk and folds his hands under his chin, his gaze never leaving her.

Cheyenne takes a breath and exhales.

"I visited a church here twenty years ago when I was young. I don't remember the name or where exactly it was located, but I can describe it fairly well. I need to know where I can find it and then make arrangements to go there." She smiles weakly. "The sooner the better," she adds hastily. "It's quite important."

"Of course," the manager says with a grin. He has been studying the outline of her breasts behind the thin rayon and is in love with what he sees. He reaches for the pen in his breast pocket and suspends it over the pad. "Please tell me what you recall. Be as specific as possible."

Cheyenne does her best to recall the church where she and Taj were interrogated. The details are of course ancient and fuzzy, but they bubble to the surface quickly.

"I know it had a tall steeple with a cross on top. And there was this dome for a roof. I remember the smooth curve of the dome," she says excitedly. "Oh, and there's a small cemetery off to the side, inside a brick courtyard. Does that help?" she asks, biting her lip.

Ever since she made the decision an hour ago to meet her fears head on, she has known what she needs to do, and where to start. Seeing the mother and daughter together on the beach brought it home for her. Much of what Cheyenne has resisted and kept buried for all these years has to do with her mamma.

In a sense, she's traveled here, all of this way, not for herself, not for Taj, but for her mother. And for all of the things that have been left unsaid between them. She understands this now. And Cheyenne knows where she needs to venture in order to finish this, once and for all.

The hotel manager's gape steals away from her for a moment (a chore, no doubt, but Cheyenne ignores the glare) as he sweeps his gaze up toward the ceiling to consider her description. He makes a few notes before picking up the phone and dialing a number. When it is answered, he shifts into a rapid-fire patois heavy with a brogue that Cheyenne has little chance of following. He speaks for three to five minutes, asking questions, listening, and writing on the legal pad before putting the phone down and eyeing her with a grin.

"Good news!" he exclaims. "My grand mama is a God-fearing woman—been one all her life. *And . . .*" he pauses for effect before continuing, "she knows this island better than anyone alive. Grand mama knows *precisely* which church you refer to!"

Cheyenne's eyes light up but the words to her response catch in her throat. She nods instead.

"It's only about a forty- to fifty-minute drive from here. Some dirt roads but nothing a truck or Land Rover can't handle." He refolds his hands under his chin and displays a satisfied look.

"That is wonderful." She eyes his name tag, "*Rodney*! You are most efficient—most efficient indeed!" She blushes and Rodney the manager is hooked. "But where can I find a truck with such little notice?"

Rodney sits up erectly and slightly lifts his chin.

"You are in luck, madam," he says proudly.

"I happen to own a 1975 Land Rover. I am restoring it myself. The only one on the island!" he exclaims arrogantly. "And it would be my pleasure if you would allow me to take you there!"

Cheyenne clasps her hands together providing ample exposure of her cleavage.

"That, Rodney, would be *so* wonderful. But I assume you need to stay here and work, and I really . . ."

"Oh no," Rodney interrupts, proudly, "give me an hour to finish up some things here and change. Then we can head out."

"Oh that would be lovely. Thank you so much!"

Cheyenne is thinking about the drive ahead and just what she will do when she gets there.

They emerge from the forest three hours shy of twilight. Taj is exhausted but feels liberated. He had allowed the details of his fall from the sky and subsequent torture by the madman, Seifu, to run their course, like a potent strain of flu that is not susceptible to medication—only time would heal those wounds.

For years he had refused to pick at those lesions for fear that they would never mend. And there was the pact that Cheyenne and Taj made to conceal their experience. Taj was not one to go back on his word.

No. He kept the horrid details of his capture hidden from everyone—family, schoolmates, and even other church members. They had agreed that this way was best. Better for both of them to get on with their lives—they had a great deal for which to be thankful. They were the *survivors*—they needn't dwell on the past or on things that cannot be changed. Best to bury those things that are harmful.

Nicole, his soul mate—the woman whom he had chosen to be his wife, had no inkling what had transpired. What would Nicole do if she knew the truth?

Taj wondered if Cheyenne's husband was incognizant as well.

In a sense, Taj was living a lie. He and Cheyenne both were. That was a sobering thought that made his step falter.

The jeep remains where they had left it earlier. Frankie takes the packs and slings them in the back as Taj walks past the wide steps and toward the cemetery. He passes an aging Land Rover parked to the right of the entrance on the edge of the dirt road—forest green in color with a safari-like rack bolted to the roof. It needs work, Taj can see, but then again, they are in Jamaica, and parts for an English car are undoubtedly difficult to find.

Frankie lights a cigarette and watches Taj

enter the cemetery through a brick archway covered with a maze of tangled vines. He steers away from the main plots. The ground here is uneven; the soil grips headstones that have been weathered by countless storms and old age. Near the corner of the courtyard where the brick is beginning to decay and flake, Taj comes to rest by two graves, wiping the sweat from his brow as he reads the inscriptions.

He feels his heart rate increase—feels the tension rise like mercury in a thermometer—temperature rising, sizzling heat. A breath, hot on his neck, tickles his senses. Taj spins around, only to find no one there.

Stop it, Taj tells himself. There is no reason to be afraid. He takes a breath and bows his head, forcing himself to stare at the inscriptions, reading every word, noting each hand-chiseled symbol in the stone.

Let it go, he instructs the synapses that control his actions. There are a million things that can now be said; he has considered a dozen of them while anticipating this moment. But as he stares down at the windswept and slanting slabs of stone, he realizes that whatever he says no longer matters.

The dead can no longer hear him.

Besides, how do you apologize for taking a life?

* * *

Taj's boots crunch on the gravel by the side of the road as he makes his way back to the jeep. Frankie, pulling on his third cigarette of the afternoon, spies Taj out of the corner of his eye, flicks the butt to the ground, and crushes it with his toe.

"Everyting irie, boss?" Frankie asks in his native slang.

"Everyting irie," Taj mimics and smiles. He opens the jeep door and climbs inside.

Frankie asks, "Not going back inside?" as he gestures with his thumb to the top step of the church.

Taj shakes his head. Frankie shrugs, gets in, and cranks the engine. The jeep is placed in gear, hand brake released, and Frankie steers the vehicle past the Land Rover to a dirt turn-around adjacent to the tree line. He U-turns the vehicle and accelerates past the entrance, sending gravel and dust into a widening plume behind them.

Taj is already facing forward. His mind is clear—a clean slate, like a freshly washed class-room chalkboard. Frankie steers them onto the road that will lead them away from this place that has haunted Taj for two decades.

And right before the bend in the road, Taj pivots in his seat for one final glance at the church—*their sanctuary, their calm after the storm*—to record the image one last time. The thick oak door opens, yet Taj cannot hear the groan under the squealing tires and crunch of gravel. A hand grasps the edge of the stained wood for support.

The shock of frizzy cinnamon hair arrests his heart.

"Back up," Taj roars to his driver. "BACK THIS THING UP NOW!"

Frankie brings the jeep to a screeching halt. He throws it in reverse and floors the gas pedal. Hearing the engine scream, he grips the steering wheel, focusing his entire attention on keeping the vehicle from running off the road.

Taj's gaze is locked behind them. His mouth hangs open and he is in shock. His heart is pounding so hard he doubts his chest can take it.

They whiz past the Land Rover as Frankie brakes.

Taj's door is already opened, missing the Rover's side molding by mere inches. Before the jeep can screech to a halt Taj is out, boots scraping the ground as he flings himself toward the steps.

Cheyenne has emerged from the church's interior and is descending the steps with Rodney in tow. She spots Taj in mid-stride.

Her mouth contours like a donut as she zeros in on his eyes—those hazel eyes.

"Look into my eyes . . ."
"Oh my God," she manages to murmur.
Cheyenne leaps for the bottom step.
Taj bolts for the top step.
Somewhere in the middle, old friends meet.

Twenty-One

Words cannot convey how Taj and Cheyenne feel. Sometimes silence is best.

The two stand holding each other tightly, his arms wrapped around her body drawing her in, her arms encircling his waist, as though they might lose each other if they dared to let go. After what seems an eternity, Taj loosens his grip and Cheyenne steps back. They stare into each other's eyes. It is Cheyenne who breaks the silence first.

"My God—Taj, I never thought I'd see you again." She gazes up at him as the warmth from his eyes infuses her like hot breath into cold hands. "I never thought that I would be blessed with seeing you again. Someone must think there is some unfinished business between the two of us." She raises an eyebrow and smiles.

Taj is silent as he mulls over her words.

She is correct. There *is* business left unfinished between them. "Look at you!" Taj exclaims. "Where to begin? I have so much that I want to share with you, and of course, a million questions."

"Same here."

Rodney is standing respectfully behind her. He moves closer, extending his hand to Taj.

"Oh, forgive me," Cheyenne says. "Rodney here is from my hotel. He was gracious enough to drive me here." Taj shakes his hand.

"And that fine gentleman over there is my driver and guide, Frankie."

Frankie is standing by the jeep, his stare locked on Cheyenne. He waves to her while grinning, and nods to Rodney.

There is a moment of awkward silence among the four of them. What to do next?

Taj says, "Well, how did you find this place?"

"I recalled it from memory. There have been many details that have emerged from my foggy recollection since I saw you in New York. And, I've known for a long time that this is someplace I needed to revisit. I just was waiting for the strength to come back. Seeing you made me realize that it was finally time."

"I know. I've felt the same way. For a long, long time."

Taj takes her hand and they walk away from their drivers.

"Have you gone back?" Cheyenne asks Taj quietly. "Have you returned to the . . . crash site?"

"Yes."

"I need to go. Will you take me there?" she asks cautiously.

"Yes, of course. It's changed, yet remains the same."

"I need to finish my journey."

"I understand," Taj says. "Where are you staying?"

"Jamaican Grande, Ocho Rios. You?"

"On the southern side of the island about forty minutes from here."

Cheyenne is thinking. "Let me send my driver back. There is no need for both of them to be here."

"Agreed. Frankie can take you wherever you need to go."

Taj turns and makes eye contact with his driver. He gestures him over and explains what they intend to do.

"No problem, mon!" Frankie says, thankful for the opportunity to drive the beautiful lady around.

Cheyenne returns to the church entrance to talk with Rodney. He had hoped to spend more time with Cheyenne and is visibly disappointed. She offers to pay him for his time, but Rodney will not hear of such a thing.

"No, madam, I will not accept payment from

you. I've enjoyed our short time together. Perhaps, when you are . . . finished here, we can . . . I can be of further service to you during your stay at our hotel."

"Do you have a card, Rodney?" she asks.

He hands her one. "My private number and cell phone are listed on back, so you can get in touch with me any time of day or night."

"Thank you. I won't forget this, and you will be the one I call should I need anything else. I promise you that." The smile that she flashes warms Rodney's heart; its radiance is enough to fuel him for the drive back to the hotel.

Taj speaks with Frankie and tells him they are going back to the crash site—Frankie offers to accompany them, but Taj tells him that is unnecessary.

"Wait for us here or come back in a couple of hours. I'll need you to take us either back to my hotel or to hers."

Frankie nods, the sparkle of a precious gem in his eyes.

"Aye Chief!" he says, giving him a mock salute, "Frankie does exactly what you says!"

Taj sits in the shade of a palm tree, his ankles resting on the cool ground. He watches her silently.

Cheyenne stands in front of the cabin with its lanky vines and tarnished skin. She has circled it several times—knelt down to stare into the dark interior. She has deliberated crawling through the maze of vegetation and undergrowth to reach the place where they spent those dreaded evenings, in those seats that seemed to fold around them and contain them—a prison—but she lacks the courage to go inside alone.

She has gone to the clearing and let her gaze sweep the forest floor that confined them so many years ago, circling the area so not to miss any details, allowing the memories to flood her consciousness. She stands now in front of Taj shaking her head. It takes her several minutes of awed silence to articulate her feelings.

"It's so weird, being here. I find it surreal. A part of me thought I'd never return to this spot—but here I am. And standing next to you. My savior."

Taj lowers his head.

Sensing his discomfort, she moves away to a distance not far from the cabin. She points down and says softly, "This is where it occurred, you know. Right next to the fire. This is where he forced me to lie down."

Taj stands, brushes the dust from his shorts and legs, and goes to her. He touches her shoulder.

"You don't need to do this, Jazz," he says softly.

She turns to him. "Do you remember how

those words of yours soothed me? Do you know that they kept me sane?"

Taj glances away.

"They did. Every time that *fucker* raped me, it was your words and your eyes that calmed me; you kept me from disintegrating, breaking apart like . . ." her words faltered as tears spilled, "like our airplane."

Taj comforts her as his palm softly makes circular motions on Cheyenne's back and shoulders.

"It was because of me that he got out of the cockpit alive. If I hadn't rescued him then . . ."

Cheyenne turns abruptly to him. "Don't do this, Taj," she says. "Don't you dare take responsibility for anything he did! His actions were his own doing. That fucker was sick—deranged."

Cheyenne pauses in remembrance as Taj shakes his head.

"I could have stopped him . . ." he says quietly, head bowed low. "Because of me you suffered as long as you did."

"NO!" she exclaims, reaching for his face. "No, Taj—you saved us. You saved me! Because of you, we are alive!"

She glances back at the decrepit cabin encircled by deformed finger-like vines. And she remembers . . .

Taj sprang from the cabin entrance like a grasshopper, catching him off guard. Before Seifu had time to react, the stick arced sideways from the concealed space behind Taj's back, connecting with Seifu's shoulder.

Taj had aimed for the head, but Seifu had shifted out of the way.

The blow knocked him to the ground. He reached behind for his blade, but Taj hammered down on him with the stick, connecting stick-to-flesh with a sickening thud. Seifu flinched and cried out.

Taj had a crazed look on his face, and Seifu for the first time felt fear. He saw in those eyes something he had not seen in Taj before.

Indifference.

Taj no longer cared if he lived or died. And that made Taj extremely dangerous.

Cheyenne, too, was out of the cabin, a stick in her hand. Seifu's eyes widened as she swung at him as if she held a golf club. The wood connected with the side of his head and blood flew from Seifu's mouth. He tried to scream, but no sound emerged. Seifu rolled over on his side as the pain ballooned inside him.

Taj lifted the stick over his head again and was preparing to strike when Seifu lashed out for Cheyenne. He succeeded in grabbing her ankle and twisted violently, sending her careening to the ground. She screamed as Taj pummeled him in the chest with the stick. The wind was knocked out of him, but he held onto Cheyenne, managing to twist himself over onto his stomach and yank her toward him.

She kicked and screamed, batting him on the

shoulders with her stick. Seifu snatched it from her; before Taj could react, Seifu was on top of her, the wood at her throat.

His words were flames that spit in their direction. He screamed and cursed their names, ear-splitting reverberations, as he pressed his weight down on Cheyenne's neck, determined to squeeze the last bit of life out of her.

He was succeeding.

But Taj stopped him, beating Seifu with the stick from behind, as if he were chopping wood. A steady stream of unintelligible words spurted from Taj's lips as he swung hard and low.

Seifu was invincible, seeming to grow stronger with every blow. Taj jumped on top of his back, attempting to reach for the blade that was still sheathed. Sensing this strategy, Seifu moved skillfully, causing Taj to lose his balance. The stick was knocked to the ground as Taj skidded across Seifu's back.

Cheyenne's eyes were bulging and her face was turning blue. She flailed her arms, but they were like mosquitoes that landed on Seifu's forearms—he merely brushed them aside.

Taj regained his footing and stood; using all of his strength he kicked Seifu in the side of the head. The boot connected and Taj felt the crunch and knew that this time he had done some damage. Seifu landed on his back. His arms were at his side and his bloodshot eyes rolled back in his head. For a moment, thankfully, he was still.

Taj went to Cheyenne who was nearly unconscious and dragged her toward the cabin by her shoulders. He glanced away for a second. That was all Seifu needed.

Taj saw the gleam before it actually registered.

By then it was too late.

The blade was speeding toward his face. Taj scrambled to his feet and ducked away—the blade caught him in the forearm and sliced deep into his flesh. Taj cried out and swung around frantically searching for a stick—for any weapon. He pivoted and saw Seifu lunge from his position. Seifu, once again defying physics with his movement, flew toward Taj like Superman, the gleaming blade locked in his dark fist. Taj crashed into the cabin's wall as he backed up instinctively, the razor-sharp metal zeroing in on him. He lost his balance and fell to the ground.

Seifu was like a bullet—on track and on target. He barreled forward and could not be stopped.

Then Seifu saw it.

Taj reached behind him in a fluid motion, his hand emerging from his waist with a flash of metal—a jagged pointy shiv, which Taj had removed from the remains of the airplane's cabin. (It took three days to pry the metal from fuselage and hone it into shape. It wasn't pretty or very shiny, but it was functional.)

Seifu recognized it was too late.

As Seifu swiped his blade down aiming for Taj's

head, Taj bent sideways, thrusting his makeshift blade up and into Seifu's midsection with both hands. The metal caught as Seifu landed on top of Taj. Seifu screamed—the blade digging deep. Seifu's knife, missing Taj's head by meager inches, punched a hole in the fuselage and embedded itself in the cabin's wall.

Taj, using all four limbs and every ounce of force that he could muster, pushed Seifu off of him. Seifu's eyes were wide. He rolled onto the ground, the metal shiv rooted in his chest like a stalk. He sucked in a breath, making woozing sounds as he struggled on the ground.

Taj's chest was heaving and he was shaking terribly. His gaze swept to Cheyenne who remained where she lay, not moving. He ran to her, mindful of Seifu, and shook her shoulders. Her eyes fluttered open and she coughed violently, her entire body wracked with spasms.

Seifu had rolled over and was curling himself into a ball. After a moment he mustered the strength to sit up, slowly. His eyes were bloody and blazed with hatred.

"Yu kill me, Taj Mahal, yu and dat fuck Norie— du it now!" Seifu tried to spit blood but it just flowed over his bruised lip and down his chin. His chest was an expanding canvas of crimson. His eyes swept down to his wound and the embedded metal, then back up at Taj. Amazement filled his eyes.

"Kill me, Taj Mahal—use dat knife dere—da wun me shudda cut yur devil eyes out wid."

Taj glanced slowly over to the blade and reached for the handle, resting his hand on it before pulling. The blade slid out of the cabin wall with a screech.

"Seifu, I should have killed you long ago," Taj seethed. His left arm hung limp and blood streamed from the wound, splattering the earth.

Seifu grinned, displaying bloody, broken teeth.

"Du it, yung brudder, be de man and finish wat yu start!" Seifu coughed but miraculously held himself up.

Taj tightened the grip on the blade. He moved toward Seifu, raising the knife. When he was a few feet away, he held it high over his head and peered down, his eyes mere slits. Seifu was silent.

All thoughts, feelings, and emotions of the plane crash and their subsequent horrific peregrination coursed through Taj's veins. He felt himself growing hot, then hotter as the flames licked him from within until he was burning with fever. The pain struck him in the temple, shooting through his body like lightning, synchronously energizing and damaging. His hand quaked as he held the heavy blade over his head.

God forgive me, he thought, the anger seething from his pores. He wanted this man dead so badly that he could taste the bile on his tongue. Taj exhaled forcefully and dropped his hand as his eyes flickered up a millimeter.

Seifu saw the momentary distraction and began to turn his head. In that second, he heard the guttural cry, a scream that erupted from deep within *the epicenter of Cheyenne's being. The stick that Cheyenne held tightly between her hands crashed into his jaw, shattering the left side of his face.*

Two things then occurred simultaneously—Seifu's body swept toward the ground, and the blade fell from Taj's hand, both as if in slow motion. The knife struck the earth without a sound and its pointed blade dug deep, embedding itself in the soft brown soil. And Seifu came to rest close by, his vacant, lifeless orbs reflecting the flash of sunlight that ricocheted off the knife's surface. The wind whistled through the trees, causing limbs to quiver and dance from the breeze's hypnotic touch.

He is a killer.

The realization clobbers him dead in the chest, knocking the wind from him. It causes him to hang his head low, but not close his eyes. Taj keeps them open in order to stare at his hands—dark skin on large fingers, veins showing—hands that took the life of a man—hands that stopped a beating heart . . .

Taj stares at the spot where it occurred. And he, like Cheyenne, remembers it all. For the first time in twenty years, he does not turn from what he feels, nor does he sense the pang that usually lives deep in his gut.

Coming here was the first step. Coming back to the very spot where he took the life of his captor, stopping him from continuing his reign of carnage that was slowly wringing the life out of Cheyenne and in the end would have killed Taj, too, has made him realize that he did what he had to do.

The ground is dark, but Taj does not see the blood—twenty years of sun, storms, and age have obliterated what erupted from Seifu when he connected with Taj's makeshift blade. His blood runs deep. Fresh soil and brown leaves cover it up.

He did what he had to do. Cheyenne has helped him see that.

Cheyenne goes to him, touches his shoulder.

"Because of you we live. Thank you, Taj."

Taj turns to study her features.

"The Bible says it's wrong to kill a man. Do you know that?"

"Yes," she says quietly.

Taj scans the canopy above him. "My father raised me to do what is right. I was in church before I could walk—can't imagine a life without my faith. And yet I went against everything I had been taught—something so deeply profound as killing a man . . ."

"Taj," Cheyenne interrupts softly, "I can only imagine what you have gone through—I know that guilt and shame eat away at you. But you need to know that God is not angry with you for what you did here. He is not looking down with a frown. Just the opposite—he is smiling. You are a savior."

He turns to stare at her. "I am no savior."

"Taj—he would have killed us!" she exclaimed, coming to stand directly in front of him. "Do you understand that? Without question Seifu was going to kill us—you and me— it was in those crazed eyes as plain as day. You did what you had to do. We both did. And I don't regret for one moment how things ended. And you shouldn't either.

"Because of you we live."

Taj nods silently. He glances back at the patch of earth where Seifu breathed his final breath, curled up in a fetal position, the blade that sliced his heart in two embedded in his thick chest—slowing that poisoned heart to death. And Taj finds peace among those dark leaves that stir gently, commanded by an unseen wind.

He knows Cheyenne is right.

He did what he needed to do.

Seifu got what he deserved.

Taj glances up, feeling the sunlight bathe his skin with its warmth.

Cheyenne is right. God is not frowning on him.

* * *

"There is one final thing I need to do," Cheyenne says softly, wiping away the tears from her face.

"I know." Taj, too, has been crying. Together, they stand by the wreckage, holding each other as the sobs wrack their bodies, allowing the feelings that had been dormant for so many years to bubble to the surface. Through their silence, together and separately, they relive that last day as captives—when they banished their subjugator, the disturbed Seifu, to the only place that he deserved to inhabit—hell.

Taj steps back and stares at Cheyenne. Myriad emotions flood through him—he has so much he wants to share with this woman standing before him. But now is not the time or the place.

He prays there will be time. Later.

Cheyenne composes herself and leads them away from the clearing. She knows where she is going. She does not need a compass or a guide. The destination is one she committed to memory twenty years ago.

Taj had cradled Cheyenne's head in his lap as she lay there bleeding. She was alive and breathing, but barely. She couldn't speak, her throat severely bruised from the punishment Seifu had inflicted. The two remained on the ground, only several yards away from the cabin and Seifu's lifeless body—both refusing to turn their heads for even an instant—lest he rise and beat them again.

Finally, the realization hit home—Seifu was dead—he was finally dead and would not get up. He would no longer be able to hurt either of them again.

Taj stood, wrapping his dirty tee shirt about his forearm to stem the bleeding. He needed water—they both did. The nearest stream was fifteen minutes away. He told Cheyenne he would return shortly.

"Please, Taj. Please don't leave me here. I don't want to remain with . . . him."

Taj understood. "I know, but you need water—we both do. I'll only be a short time." He helped her to the cabin's interior, settling her into a chair and giving her a stick for insurance, just in case.

It made her feel better.

Taj returned forty minutes later. He had cleaned his wound, then rewrapped and crudely bandaged his arm using the shirt. He carried water back for Cheyenne in a container that they had found on the plane.

She was dozing peacefully when he returned. He fed her water and gave her some berries for nourishment before heading out again.

There was something he needed to do.

Seifu had kept them from a particular area south of the cabin while in captivity. He had always made them hike north or west, never allowing them to stray from his sight. At night, Seifu would disap-

pear into the bushes, and Taj knew he was going to the location that was off-limits to them.

Why? What did that area hold?

Taj intended to find out.

He returned an hour later.

He had been crying, Cheyenne could see that.

Seifu's body lay where he had fallen. Neither would touch him.

"Taj—what's wrong?" she asked as soon as he entered the cabin.

He was silent for a moment, his eyes downcast. He was weeping softly.

"Tell me!"

He glanced up and reached for her arm.

"It concerns your mother."

Cheyenne stared for several seconds, eyes unblinking. Then she began to cry, softly as she held her head in her hands.

"I'm so sorry, Jazz."

"I want to see her," Cheyenne said quickly, standing to exit the cabin.

"No—please, Jazz. That's not a good idea," Taj said. He held her close. "She's been out there for a while. I don't want you to see her like that."

"She's my mamma—I have to see her one last time." Cheyenne brushed past Taj and stood defiantly by the cabin's exterior. There was hatred in her eyes as she glared down at Seifu.

"He knew, didn't he? That fucker knew all this time!"

"Yes."

Cheyenne pivoted around fluidly to Taj who was standing behind her.

"How do you know?"

"His cigar—I found his cigar by her. I suspect he knew for a while. He hid it from us—hid it from you."

Cheyenne glared at Taj for a moment before turning slowly to Seifu. Taj could see the abhorrence blazing through her. She clenched her fists and, without warning, kicked at Seifu with all of her might. Her foot struck his side causing his body to jerk from the impact.

"You knew," she screamed at Seifu's lifeless form, "you fucking knew!"

Cheyenne kicked him again until Taj pulled her gently away.

"You bastard," she whimpered as Taj led her away, "you fucking bastard."

They arrive at the site twenty minutes later. The hike had not been difficult, and Taj found it enjoyable and therapeutic. They had both been silent with their own thoughts, respectful of the other's emotions.

There is a small clearing at the base of a rising meadow. In the distance is the ridge of the majestic Blue Mountains; behind them, an enormous oak with huge limbs and a thick base towers over them. Its limbs extend outward, sheltering the clearing with its canopy.

Some of the limbs are crooked and mis-shaped, giving the impression that the tree is decrepit and sick—but that is not the case—it is a magnificent old tree—one that has weathered countless seasons.

The clearing is mottled in shade and is cool. The damp earth is strewn with leaves. By the base of the oak is a raised plot of darkened soil. A smooth bluish-gray headstone with a deep-set inscription marks this resting place. At the foot of the plot stands a cross, constructed from several narrow tree limbs; the bark has been scraped off with a sharp blade—Seifu's knife. Twine binds the two pieces of wood together, and even after twenty years, it still holds, although the cross no longer stands straight.

This is the final resting place of Cheyenne's mother.

Cheyenne approaches it slowly. Taj remains in the background, out of reach. As he stares at the grave, he recollects how he dug the grave by hand, using only primitive utensils he had found in the cabin.

It took him two days, and he would not allow Cheyenne to assist.

She had grown weaker, the blood that she had lost coupled with her injuries from the beatings had sapped whatever strength she had left. He knew they had to leave this place soon or they would die. There was no question about that.

Together they had dragged her mother's corpse to this spot, laying her to rest in the dank earth on a spotless day.

And here they were—twenty years later, coming back to pay their respects to someone who had never been given a chance. An innocent bystander who became collateral damage in the personal war of a single demented individual.

She didn't have to die.

And they didn't have to suffer.

But they did.

Cheyenne kneels and allows her fingers to mingle with the soft earth. She closes her eyes and lets the tears flow. But they are short and brief. Lately she has cried so much she has few tears left.

"Mamma—forgive me for not returning."

Her body shakes as she tells how sorry she is. For two decades Cheyenne has been unable to come back to this place, this small clearing where her mother lies, unable to kneel before her to touch the damp earth—her earth, because of the terror that coursed through her veins every time she thought about making the somber journey.

Cheyenne was petrified of what she might find. And as the years progressed, she allowed herself to drift farther apart from the truth— that her mamma wasn't frowning down on her because Cheyenne made it out of the woods alive, and she had not.

Cheyenne never knew until now.

For the next twenty minutes Cheyenne converses with her mother. Not the one-way talks that had consumed her life: the countless times she knelt before her bed to pray and ask for her mother's guidance; the pleasant events that caused her to glance upward and wish that her mamma were there; when the enormous guilt weighed so heavily that she found herself begging her mother's forgiveness for abandoning her so—leaving her, all those years, alone, in a lifeless forest.

This time, though, Cheyenne's mamma is with her. She can feel it in the wind that whistles through the trees, in the texture of the air that envelops her as she views the grave, and in the blades of sunlight that pierce through the trees at jagged angles, beaming down on her, providing warmth and comfort.

Her mamma is here.

And so, Cheyenne talks of her life and how it has turned out. She tells her mamma that despite what she endured, she turned out okay. She has a wonderful husband, a beautiful house, a satisfying career, and close friends. No children—that is no longer possible. But life has turned out well—Cheyenne has been blessed.

Like the mother and daughter strolling along the beach, the conversation is not rushed or strained. Just two women sharing a deep-seated love and a strong bond that can never be broken. Cheyenne is elated. She feels the weight lifted from her shoulders as they converse.

She has been forgiven. Her mamma understands.

As Taj packed the last of the dirt into the ground and stuck the cross deep, Cheyenne stepped back and sank to the ground, too weak to stand. Taj came behind her and touched her shoulders. He led them in a short prayer—for her mother—and for the hope that they would make it out safely.

Afterward, he pulled Cheyenne to him and stared into her eyes.

"Jazz—listen to me," he said as the tears dried onto her cheeks. "We need to make a pact that no matter what happens, we will go forward from this place and never look back. We are survivors, you and I. We have made it. We are winners—a vital life stands before us. We can choose to live it to the fullest, taking that which is due to us, or we can dwell on our past and let it suck us down into the muck and mire of despair.

"We can't let that happen. That would not be fair. Not to ourselves, not to our families, and lastly, not to her," he said, pointing to her mother's grave.

"We can't let Seifu win. He must lose, do you hear me?"

Cheyenne nodded solemnly.

"So let's make a pact that we will put this horrible incident behind us—keep it locked away tight—forever. Let's not talk about it. Let's not dwell on it. Let's go forth from this moment with our eyes only on our glorious future—never on the horrific past . . ."

Taj took her hands in his. "Jazz, let us both live. This is a gift . . ."

Cheyenne cried silently for a moment before she wiped the tears away with her forearm. She nodded at Taj.

"Yes, Taj—I want to live. I want to rid myself of this place and never ever come back."

She glanced back at her mother's grave before turning back to Taj.

"Take me from here, Taj. Take me from this damned place so that I can live again!"

There was no ceremony before they left the camp—no last-minute prayer, no bowing of heads, no handholding. They took what they could carry and headed out. As they passed the clearing, Cheyenne, who held on to Taj for support, paused and turned back toward the cabin.

"There's one thing I need to do," she said as she headed for the aircraft that had been their jail cell.

"What?" Taj yelled behind her, dropping the packs and running toward her.

She reached the camp and stopped by the smoldering fire. The thin tendrils of smoke meandered toward the sky. Cheyenne stoked it with some kindling that had been piled up close by, and the fire began to crackle and spark.

Taj watched her curiously.

Seifu's black walking stick leaned against the hull of the cabin, its smooth surface menacing. Cheyenne grabbed it and without ritual threw it in the fire. It took a moment to catch, but Taj could see the flames that began to eat through the dark wood. She watched the stick burn.

"Fuck this wretched walking stick of his," she hissed, hobbling past Taj and leaving the campsite without glancing back.

Twenty-Two

The sunset in Ocho Rios is a dazzling display of nature's brilliance—so much so that Taj and Cheyenne decide to observe it silently. Taj takes her hand in his. They stand on the beach, both scrubbed clean by tingling, hot water—Taj clad in off-white linen pants, yellow polo shirt, and dark sandals, all compliments of Cheyenne, who had run down to the hotel shop while he showered in her room. He had been adamant about not being able to accept the clothes, finally giving way to keeping them, but saying that he would be forced to reimburse her. Cheyenne waved him away, saying it was the least she could do, and for him to consider them a gift.

Cheyenne's washed her hair and it hangs free. She looks radiant in a beige dress with spaghetti straps and low heels. The setting sun catches her in a special way—the light reflects off of her smooth, caramel skin in a manner that creates a stirring in him.

He tells her how beautiful she looks. Cheyenne stares at him for a moment before kissing him on the cheek and remarking just how handsome Taj has grown up to be. They walk back to the hotel to get something to eat. Both are famished, the excitement of the day finally catching up with them.

Over a meal of fresh seafood and a bottle of excellent Chilean Chardonnay, they talk about their lives that have taken shape and flourished since the horror they shared twenty years ago. They discuss their respective careers, Cheyenne's marriage to Malcolm and her life in southern California, Taj's engagement to Nicole and their lives in Washington, his pop, and of course, the church. It is a good conversation between old friends who have fallen out of touch but are desperate to catch up, anxious to integrate back into each other's lives.

Cheyenne feels wonderful. The past six hours have been like a godsend. She never expected to see Taj again, never expected that she would find him at the end of her rainbow—the place where she traveled to make peace with her mother.

Taj feels a calming sensation embrace him as well—he is ecstatic to see Cheyenne again; it is like icing on the cake after his long, arduous task. For two decades Taj kept a terrible secret and the guilt that accompanied it locked away, deep inside—he was a killer. But Cheyenne has helped him see that what he did was noble and courageous—that killing Seifu was their only way out, and by doing so he had liberated them and set them free.

Taj sees that now. He gets it.

And his heart and spirit can once again sail free . . .

He stares across the table at Cheyenne, whose hair is being caressed by the gentle night breeze. The stirring that he feels is welling up inside him. It has been there since he arrived back at the hotel, a dull ache, ever-present yet pleasurable. As he toweled off in her bathroom he inhaled the scents of her perfume. And now, sitting across from her, the light shimmering and sparkling in her eyes and her hair dancing with the wind as wisps of her scent invade his nostrils, he feels the desire grow. Expanding like a shockwave inside of him, he is fearful of where this may lead.

Cheyenne has stopped talking and has reached across the table to take his hand.

"Penny for your thoughts," she says with a smile.

Taj pauses. "I'm . . . just thinking . . ."

"I can see that. But I was hoping for some details."

Taj's words are a whisper. "I'm trying to decipher what I'm feeling."

She smiles. "And what are you feeling?"

He returns her smile. "I'm not sure I'm ready to share that with you just yet."

"Hmmm, I don't see why not—it's not like we're strangers. We're practically lovers." Cheyenne has a seductive smile painted on her face that Taj finds incredibly stimulating despite feeling apprehensive. She has a way of slicing through the noise—the extraneous matter—to the heart of what is most important in a way that is direct, but not overbearing. Her words are laced with delicious *possibilities*—and it's those possibilities that Taj sees now as he stares at her.

"You always had a way of saying what was on your mind," he remarks. "I've always loved that about you."

The words slipped out effortlessly and without conscious thought before Taj could even consider the implications.

Cheyenne is silent—processing those words— that word in particular—*love*. She continues with her hypnotic smile.

"What else do you *love* about me, Taj?" she asks, innocently.

Another pregnant pause.

"How about we change the subject?" he suggests, flashing his straight white teeth.

"Okay, but I thought we were sharing," she muses with a feigned look of hurt on her face.

They stare at each other—both silent with their own thoughts that swirl inside their minds like creamy batter in a mixing bowl.

"It's your eyes that I love," Cheyenne says, pushing a bit deeper.

Taj smiles. "So I've heard."

The two of them are enjoying this little game, flirting and teasing, stepping up the pressure by grasping at the faucet handle and giving it a quick spin—a bit more water with every turn . . .

But then Taj senses the change in Cheyenne—and sees her expression shift—the temperature drops and Taj is suddenly afraid.

"What's wrong?" he asks.

Cheyenne shakes her head unhurriedly, her mind locked on a new train of thought.

"May I ask you a question?" she asks. Without waiting for the answer continues, "Why didn't you stay in touch with me after . . . after our ordeal?"

Taj is silent. He knew this issue would be raised, sooner or later . . .

He sighs heavily and dips below the waves.

* * *

"How do I say this without your taking it the wrong way?" Taj ponders, his hand on his bald head.

"Why don't you say what's on your mind—what is the truth," she responds, watching him.

She sips her glass of Chardonnay as he begins.

Six months had passed since their terrible ordeal. They had been reunited with their families, and life for the most part had gone back to the way it had been—normal.

They had made it out of the forest together one brilliantly lit day, six days after their plane went down—Taj bearing the weight of Cheyenne on his back because she was too weak to walk on her own. It had taken some time—a full day of hiking away from the crash site, traveling in a widening arc of circles, until they had, by nothing short of a miracle or a sixth sense, made their way to the forest's edge and spotted the lone church beyond.

When Taj had laid Cheyenne on the ground, they were both near exhaustion and still bleeding from their wounds. He crawled up the stone steps and banged on the imposing oak doors before collapsing into near unconsciousness. The rest was like a dream—bits and pieces interspersed, some real, some imagined.

An elderly Jamaican pastor heard Taj's pound-

*ing and answered the door. When he spied Taj's
condition he wasted no time in summoning the police and medical care.*

*Cheyenne's wounds were dealt with first; she had
lost a great deal of blood and the doctor who tended
to her was deeply concerned. Besides the obvious lacerations and tearing from Seifu's stick, she had possible internal damage as well. After they were
stabilized and provided with a meal of solid food
(the first real food they'd eaten in a week), a large
uniformed man indicated that a search party had
combed the area for several days. He interrogated
them with questions that seemed to go on forever. Finally, Taj refused to answer any more until he and
Cheyenne were allowed to sleep.*

*Later, after he was well rested and clean, he led
them to the wreckage and the bodies of Seifu, the
pilot, and Cheyenne's mother. They asked again how
each had been killed.*

Taj was silent.

*The church mission was notified, as was Taj's
pop and Cheyenne's stepfather, and the mission's
pastor was brought in to assist. In the end, their
wounds healed and they were sent home, quietly
and without commotion. The uniformed man with
the brass buttons informed them that they would be
well compensated for their pain and suffering.*

*It would be months before they fully understood
what that meant. By the time Cheyenne and Taj
were reunited in Philadelphia six months later (a
trip coordinated by the church), both families had*

received enough money to pay for college and any outstanding medical bills.

The money couldn't bring Cheyenne's mother back.

Seifu and the pilot were buried in the northeast corner of the church's cemetery. Based on the wishes of Cheyenne's family, a headstone would be erected but her mother's grave would remain where they had buried her.

All of these years . . .

Taj recalls the anticipation of seeing Cheyenne after six months—was she fully healed? What would she think of him now? And what would they say to each other? He had no idea what to expect.

His pop had accompanied him to Philly, a trip made possible by the generosity of the church. They had assembled at Cheyenne's church for the service—the two families meeting together for the first time—Taj and his pop, Cheyenne and her stepfather, and their respective pastors. Cheyenne's physical wounds had healed quite nicely. Taj remembers spotting her as they entered the church: she turned in her pew and gave him a quick wave before rushing up to hug him. He had been cognizant of all eyes on them, so he had pulled back quickly. But the hug had warmed his heart and his soul.

They did not speak at all about what had transpired between them. Their families did not possess the details—that was the deal that had been consummated back in the forest.

AWAKENING

Even Taj's pop didn't know the full circum-
stances of their ordeal.

It was better that way.

After a lengthy church service that praised the re-
union of the two young adults, they had gone back
to her stepfather's house for dinner. Taj and Chey-
enne had their first opportunity to be alone then,
taking leave of the house to stroll around the neigh-
borhood after clearing away the plates as the adults
retired to the living room for coffee.

Taj had asked Cheyenne if she were well.

And he asked if she were keeping her part of the
bargain.

Cheyenne had nodded somberly.

"That night," Taj remarks, "when you and I
were finally alone, and I was able to look at
you without feeling the weight of everyone's
eyes on me—I became overwhelmed. The
feelings and emotions that I had buried for
the past six months welled to the surface. Suddenly, I was back there, Seifu's knife at my
throat, his black walking stick between your
legs, and I felt suffocated."

"I understand," Cheyenne says softly.

"Do you?" he asks, "I don't think so. Seeing
you meant that I could not put the past behind me. Seeing you meant I would be unable
to keep my end of the bargain—our pact."

"I see," Cheyenne says, her eyes filling with mist.

"Believe me when I say I never meant to hurt you. Please don't think that I no longer wanted to see you. But the only way I knew to move forward was to leave the past behind me, and that meant not seeing you again. It would be too painful for me to do anything else."

Taj is silent for a moment. Cheyenne watches the hazel eyes rimmed with wetness.

"Does it make sense?" he asks in hushed tones.

"Yes."

Silence as the waiter clears the table. The bottle is drained into wine stems and they both take a sip.

"There is something else," Cheyenne says. "You turned down my offering."

Taj swallows hard.

"Tell me why," she pleads.

Taj recalls that night vividly—the cool breeze that covered them like a shawl—the huge oak trees that lined her street and hid the moon from their view. Only the dim light from street lamps illuminated their way. They strolled together, holding hands, enjoying the warmth from the contact and the silence that was just right, between two people who had experienced something deep and profound.

"You look well, Taj," she said, breaking the silence. "I was worried about you."

"It was I who was worried about you. Are you truly okay?" he asked her, "Please tell me that you are."

"I am. Truly."

"Do you think about it?" he asked quietly.

"Yes. I haven't learned how not to. I still wake up sometimes screaming for her—for my mamma. That's the hardest part," she whispers.

"I wish things had turned out differently," he said softly. "I wish she had made it out with us."

"I will always wish for that."

She gripped his hand tighter as they turned a corner, strolling deeper into the quiet neighborhood.

"Everyone keeps asking me if I'm okay," she said. "Everyone wants to know what really happened there. But I don't tell them."

"It's for the best."

They walked along a park whose entrance was flooded by brilliant lamplight swarming with insects and fluttering moths. She led him onto a footpath past a statue of a horse forged from bronze. The park was well kept with closely cropped grass and well-manicured shrubs. Moonlight shone down illuminating the path in front of them. She led them to a second path that took them deeper into the park. Passing a fountain that paid tribute to Benjamin Franklin, they passed several benches before selecting one that butted up against the base of a weeping willow whose branches scraped the ground. The *shadows were haunting, but neither Taj nor Chey-enne were afraid.*

Taj sat on the backrest of the bench while Chey-enne took a seat beneath him. His fingers massaged the muscles in her neck and shoulders. She closed her eyes and tilted her head back, enjoying his touch and his scent.

"Oooh, you're good—you should set up shop!" she mused as she rotated her head.

"You're just saying that!"

They were silent some more, enjoying the feeling of reuniting, and the closeness that they shared.

They had been through so much together—gone through the fire and come out, charred, but alive— sharing secrets that would bond for life.

Taj stared down at her features that were high-lighted by the moon. She was indeed beautiful, and his thoughts went back to that day in the clearing when it had poured, seeing her nude for the first time—for a brief moment, free of the chains that bound her.

His pulse quickened and he ceased kneading her shoulders.

Cheyenne glanced back.

"What's wrong?" she asked.

"Nothing." Taj could feel himself rising, a feel-ing that both excited and frightened him.

Cheyenne stood up to turn around, staring at Taj for a long time. She moved as he watched her, his eyes never straying from her face. She smiled as she leaned in and kissed him softly. It was a gentle kiss, but Taj felt the gooseflesh that rose like dorsal fins, and the current that surged through him was part pleasure, part pain.

This was something he had never experienced before.

Cheyenne moved back and stared at him, as if checking to see if he was okay.

He said nothing.

She moved in and kissed him again. This time she opened her mouth, and Taj slipped his tongue inside, tasting her for the first time, feeling the voltage increase as their tongues intertwined like vines on a tree, a dance where they both found a rhythm and grooved together. Her hands moved to his shoulders and slid down his forearms slowly to his sides, reaching around his waist as she moved further into him, feeling his quivering flesh expand.

Taj was attempting to control his breathing, but the flames that had been stoked were now burning out of control. His was a raging forest fire, uncontained . . .

Cheyenne snaked her fingers over his thighs lightly, feeling the contours of his jeans before she crept toward the space between his legs.

In that moment a rush of emotions and feelings flooded through Taj, all extraordinary, wonderfully sensual and provocative: Cheyenne pressing herself against him, her breasts that tickled his chest as she breathed, the way her tongue darted between his teeth, painting his lips with her wetness. His own flesh was fully engorged and tingling; his jeans were ready to burst from her touch.

"Oh God, Taj—you feel so good," she said, grinding her hips against him. Taj attempted to pull back and give himself some distance, but there was no place to go. He was aware of his inflamed sex that pressed into her, and he was embarrassed. He didn't want her to see him this way. He was losing control, like a drug that is consumed and takes over; he simply didn't know what to do.

"There's something I've wanted to do since Jamaica," Cheyenne said softly, her words blowing warm air against his ear. Taj was dizzy with desire, yet the apprehension was like mercury rising.

"Cheyenne," he said, gently pushing her away from him so that he could breathe, "This isn't a good idea . . ."

"Taj—I want you to have this—I need to feel you in a way that is special and sweet." She reached for his shirt and pulled it away from his jeans. Taj was processing her words, thinking about all that was sweet—Cheyenne, her silky hair between his fingers, her firm round breasts that he longed to grasp, hips and legs that he envisioned wrapping around him like a weed growing out of control, constricting him until he could no longer breathe.

Taj grabbed her hands and put a stop to her actions.

"Cheyenne," he said, breathlessly. "We can't do this."

She ignored him, running her fingers over his

chest, feeling the extended nipples and taut muscles. The feeling was so delicious that Taj felt himself slipping—standing on the edge of a great cliff, the ocean's horizon distant as his footing gives way, and he wants desperately to grab hold of something—anything, but the beautifully setting sun has his attention locked, and so he is powerless to control his destiny—he slides gracefully off the edge of rock and low brush, experiencing himself fall as he calls out for her . . .

"Please, Taj, this is a gift that I want you to have."

Taj stood up, his hands electrified as he brushed against her breasts as he moved away, fighting to control his breathing. He turned toward the willow, out of the moonlight that showcased his engorged state.

"I can't," he said softly. "We should go," he added weakly, as Cheyenne remained by the bench, the shadows from the tree concealing the tremble in her lips and the fresh tears on her cheeks.

Twenty-Three

The heavy bass of reggae draws them near. Hand in hand, Taj and Cheyenne walk barefoot over cool sand toward the music. Sandals swing from their free hands. The band is on an elevated stage that faces the open-air bar with a thatch-covered roof. Sand is the dance floor—it is filled with spinning, gyrating couples. Off to the side is a bonfire, which has been built on the beach. Its warmth is intense—loaded with logs that spit and crackle, sending up plumes of red-orange sparks.

It is Christmas Eve. Taj orders a pair of drinks, something exotic, and they toast each other silently.

Cheyenne speaks. "So, you haven't answered my question."

"I know," he says, taking another sip of his drink. "I'm not avoiding your question."

"You sure?" she muses.

"Cheyenne," Taj says, leading her to a table where they can talk without shouting over the din of music. "You are a beautiful woman— then and now. Now even more so."

Cheyenne blushes.

"I was as much attracted to you then . . ." Taj pauses, realizing he's already said too much.

"And? Don't leave that hanging. Finish your thought, Taj."

Taj sighs. "I was as much attracted to you then as I am to you *now*." He smiles at her.

"The feeling is very much mutual."

Taj nods.

"But that doesn't explain why you turned me down." Cheyenne dropped her head and lowered her voice. "Was it because you thought I was dirty? Because of what happened? Because Seifu had ruined me?"

"What?" Taj stands and peers at Cheyenne. Her eyes are misting. She dabs at them with a napkin.

"He did, you know—ruin me. And I wouldn't blame you if that was the reason."

Cheyenne is staring at Taj. A single tear meanders down her cheek.

"Oh my God, Jazz—you can't be serious."

He moves to her and wipes the tear away with his thumb. "Jazz—it wasn't that—I swear it. You aren't dirty or damaged. You're not ruined, Jazz—Seifu didn't ruin you. He made you stronger."

"I wanted you Taj. That night I wanted to make love to you so badly—I needed to feel something that was real and warm and sweet. I needed to feel what a man feels like—not some inanimate object like a walking stick!"

"Oh God. Jazz, I am so sorry," he says, taking her in his arms. He holds her tight, feeling her heartbeat as he presses against her. "I never meant for you to think that I didn't want you. It was just the opposite—I wanted you very badly, too. But I didn't know how to express it. I was afraid, Jazz. Afraid that I . . . wouldn't do . . . what I needed to do . . . to make you love me."

Cheyenne pulls back, gazing up into his eyes.

"What are you saying, Taj?" she asks, cautiously.

Taj holds her hands as he stares down into her eyes that sparkle from the firelight. He does not blink; he does not look away.

"I loved you, Jazz—I fell in love with you the moment I saw you round the corner in that rundown airport terminal with your bell bottom jeans and that flowery top."

Taj laughs as he remembers.

"Oh yes—I remember you. I remember what you were wearing, how you wore your hair—I was smitten, no question about it. And after everything that we went through—after coming through all of that and surviving, I felt a closeness to you that I can't put into words.

"Seeing you that night after six months was one of the most amazing experiences of my life. Seeing how fresh and wonderful you looked made my heart swell. And make no mistake, Jazz—I wanted you. I wanted you so badly. But the thought of messing that up, doing something wrong, seeing how I was inexperienced in those days, scared me nearly to tears. I didn't know what to do. I panicked, I froze, and I resisted."

Cheyenne is watching Taj carefully as she nods her head in understanding.

"You don't think I'm dirty?" she asks, her voice barely above a whisper.

"Oh Jazz!" he says, taking her face in his hands. Twelve inches separate them. He goes to her, watching her lips part in anticipation of the kiss that is sure to come.

They connect—their lips pressing together until their mouths open, and Taj slips his tongue inside. He savors the taste of Cheyenne—her sweetness as she presses into him, the flavor of Chardonnay on their lips as they join, the distance and time that has separated them compressing until there is nothing—

not one single particle that stands between them.

"Hey, isn't that the singer?" she hears and pulls back begrudgingly.

Taj is still staring at her lovely face as she turns toward the source of the sound: an elderly couple. The gentleman clad in Bermuda shorts, a tacky Hawaiian shirt, and an enormous cowboy hat flashes a smile. "Hey!" he says, raising a bony finger in her direction, "I know you!"

Cheyenne smiles and waves.

"Yes you do," she says, snaking her arm around Taj's waist. "These are my friends," she says to him. "We met yesterday."

"This lady sure can sing," he announces to Taj. "Remember how good she sang, honey?" he says, turning to his heavily made-up wife.

"Sure do. You gonna sing for us tonight?" his wife asks.

"Oh yeah, that would be swell," her husband adds.

Cheyenne moves closer to Taj—relishing the feeling of his body nudging hers. She bites her bottom lip.

"Umm, I don't think so," she says, her eyes flicking between Taj and the couple.

"Ah damn, sure would love to hear that pretty voice one more time!"

Taj glances down at Cheyenne and senses

her apprehension. "What's wrong?" he whispers.

"Nothing, I just don't like singing for crowds, that's all. Besides," she says, leaning into him, "I really want to kiss you again."

Taj pauses in mid-step and glances at her, grinning.

"Aw come on!" the wife pleads. "It would be so much fun. I'm sure the singers won't mind."

They walk toward the band, which has just finished a song. Taj takes Cheyenne's hand in his as the applause erupts around them. Cheyenne's heart is beating and Taj feels her grip tighten.

"You don't have to do this, you know," Taj tells her. "Although, I recall a beautiful girl with a dazzling voice—I sure would love to hear her again, Jazz."

Cheyenne stops and turns to him. She reaches for him, placing her hand on the back of his head. She brings his head to hers, pressing her lips gently against his. They kiss softly for a moment before pulling back.

Cheyenne goes to the corner of the stage and signals to the keyboard player. He comes over, his huge dreadlocks swinging like a pendulum as he leans over. They converse for a moment before Cheyenne takes to the stage.

The crowd quiets as the lights dim and the piano player is reseated. He begins to play, softly and melodically, "Love Me Still" by Chaka Khan as Cheyenne steps to the microphone.

And then she sings, the words ingrained in her mind, those lyrics that she knows like skin on the back of her hand, singing this song as if there is no audience before her—no one save for Taj—standing tall and handsome with those pretty hazel eyes, arresting eyes that tug at her heartstrings and tickle her soul. Cheyenne closes her eyes and locks in on a single thought that sustains her—the *sensation* of Taj—his scent, taste, touch, and kiss—his entire being that sweeps over her like light clouds, comforting her, making her feel clean and whole again.

Cheyenne feels a sudden release. Two decades filled with darkness: haunting memories, sad thoughts, burdens she's shouldered for twenty years, demons she has been unwilling to face . . .

But now she's feeling the warmth from the light: a mother's undying love and forgiveness, and the final self-acceptance that comes with this freedom.

Love surrounds her on all sides, fueling this warmth.

Cheyenne sings her heart out, swaying as the piano's sweet notes pierce the delightful night. Her eyes open and sweep across the crowd that gazes admiringly toward her, and find Taj who stands alone, watching her sing with a look of pure admiration and love—love for her and her craft—decorated across his face.

And when she is done—when she has sung her last note, stretched it until her voice begins to waver and she quiets herself until it's just a hair's-breadth wide, the crowd erupts with applause—thunderous claps that lift her up with their intensity; their warm smiles bathing her as they stand to give Cheyenne her due, carrying her soul heaven-bound. . . .

The breeze is delightful. It tickles their skin, gently tugs at Cheyenne's hair. They walk the beach—away from the compound, the moon casting an eerie glow on the waves that shimmer as they collide with the sandy shore.

There are no words—the unspoken chemistry between them is sufficient. Taj relishes her touch—he can't seem to get enough. His fingers are intertwined with hers, and he rubs at her digits with his thumb, feeling the soft skin that is reminiscent of glove leather.

There are dunes to their right. Silently, Taj leads her to them. They climb slowly, Taj pausing to grasp her waist, ensuring she doesn't fall. They put on their sandals, and walk over squat blades of wide grass that are coarse and uneven. Beyond them is a stand of thick trees. The blackness is like an intoxicating liqueur—

it's inviting yet they resist, walking onward, parallel to the forest.

A few hundred yards away, Taj sees a break between the trees. He steers them toward it as Cheyenne hums to herself quietly, thankful that Taj is back in her life, and that he was here to witness the break in her silence.

A thick overhang of brush and hanging branches frame their passage. Taj leads, his step steady as he carefully maneuvers around a mound of thorny shrubs. There is a clearing directly in front of them—a space perhaps twenty square feet in size. It has a rippling sand floor that is warm and cozy. Taj takes off his sandals and squishes his toes into the sand.

Cheyenne glances around. She feels an urgency—her pulse quickens and she takes in a quick breath—but Taj is there, running his palm along her back slowly, comforting her. He faces her and before she can speak, his mouth is on hers, slipping his tongue inside, relishing the taste and warmth of her. He reaches for her, pulling her into him. They nuzzle and find that space that feels perfect— her limbs settling against his, her thighs brushing against his with increased force and desire.

Taj reaches for her hands and kneels down, taking Cheyenne with him. He stretches out on the sand and pulls her on top of him. Her hair spreads across his chest as he reaches for her face, using his fingertips to lightly trace her facial lines. His fingers move downward— slowly painting a pathway from her chin to her neck, then to her clavicles and shoulder blades. He cups his hands as they reach the rise of her breasts—Cheyenne groans as Taj presses to feel her flesh. He kisses her again, taking her bottom lip between his, painting it with his wet tongue.

Cheyenne stands, backs away a few feet, and slowly unzips her dress; she stares at him, eyes unblinking as she lets it fall to the ground. Moonlight cascades down, illuminating her with light. The dress lies in a heap by her an-kles, and she steps free, turning around slowly, unbuttoning her bra as she pirouettes. When she faces him again, her breasts are free, and Cheyenne lowers her hands allowing Taj to marvel at her firm and well-sculpted body.

In the moonlight, Taj can see that her nip-ples are cherry red and taut. He sits up, and stretches to them, straining as she stands just out of reach. Her fingers catch the thin waist-band of her black g-string and pause there for a moment—toying with him as his stare is glued to her lovely form. Taj kneels and she moves closer to him, until the tops of her panties are level with his daunting eyes. She exhales slowly and begins to vibrate, shudder-ing the way a leaf flaps in an evening down-pour. Taj raises his arms, placing both hands on her navel, and slides them up, excruciatingly slow, inch by inch until they reach and glide over her breasts. He squeezes the flesh, running his index fingers over her nipples as he inhales her scent. He leans in, his face touching the laced fabric. Exhaling slowly, Taj lets his breath fan across her mound. Dropping his fingers, raking her skin as he descends, he catches her waistband and tugs, his stare riveted on the patch of exquisiteness that is unveiled.

By his hand, the g-string stretches, then falls, and Taj is face to face with her sex. It is lightly covered with hair, manicured in a way that is invigorating. She parts her legs as she grasps his shoulders for support, and Taj closes his eyes, allowing his nose to rub against the flesh of it, first to one side, then back again, taking his time, moving slowly, cognizant of her moisture that paints his skin in an increasingly wide arc.

Cheyenne groans as his tongue flicks across her epicenter. He allows it to lightly touch her lips, tasting her in the way one does a delicacy, before he probes inside. And Cheyenne cannot help but squat as she grabs his bald head, increasing her moans as he feeds upon her. His hands are on her breasts, fingers twisting her nipples which are hard and responsive. His tongue is a wild beast, sliding over her flesh, slipping inside her folds, lapping at her clitoris, sending shockwaves through her body. Cheyenne squeezes his head with both hands, guiding him inside her, rotating his face from side to side so that he cannot miss a single solitary inch, commanding his movements with her own. All the while she moans incessantly.

Taj halts his frantic activity and glances up at Cheyenne. Her eyes are glazed and she is lightheaded, already intoxicated from his potent cocktail.

Taj parts her thighs and gazes at the tattoo—the flower—jasmine, which expertly covers the raised flesh—the spot where Seifu, in an act of acute violence forever branded his mark on her. The years have softened the flesh—the edges rounded, bruising faded. Taj recalls telling her how the wound looked to be a flower—and it has metamorphosed and become one—beautiful in its lines, the grace and beauty of a living thing.

His fingers touch the spot where Seifu burned her. She is watching him. He presses his lips and then kisses it. His mouth opens and he uses his tongue to decipher its details and mysteries.

He is not afraid.

Cheyenne is beside herself—no one, not even her husband, has done that before. Then Cheyenne is on him, pushing him down onto the warm sand, straddling his legs as she reaches for his shirt and pulls it over his head in one sweeping motion. His pants come off next, and she is grabbing at his boxers and dragging them down to his ankles as his manhood, full of life, bobs around, slapping at his stomach. When he is fully naked she stands back admiring him splayed on the forest floor—this clearing that haunts her with its familiarity, but soothes and cleanses her as well. She can feel her juices flowing, emerging from her sex as she lowers herself on to him, hands to his firm chest as he passes through her slippery gate and enters her.

"Baby," Taj says, pausing to suck in a breath as his hips rise to meet hers, "Let me put on a condom . . ."

"Don't need one, lover—I can't have babies," Cheyenne says breathlessly before her hands return to his chest.

She bends down, her breasts sliding across his chest as her body covers his. She swallows up his sex, enveloping him completely, as her tongue dances inside his mouth. She grasps his head in her hands before pushing him back onto the sand.

She flexes her hips as she rides him—long, full strokes that are deep and satisfying. Taj is moaning as he holds onto her breasts tightly, her hair wriggling along her back. "Besides— I want to feel you come."

Cheyenne smiles at him, and Taj closes his eyes for a moment, savoring the feeling of her warmth that has wrapped itself around him snugly, like an oversized hand in a small glove.

They work each other—Taj meeting her thrusts with his own, until he is fatigued and has to pause. He reaches for her neck, massaging his fingers into her flesh and threading her hair between his fingers. He pulls her to him. Taj pivots underneath her and without slipping out, flips her onto her bottom. Gazing down at her lovely form, dark nipples, dark thin patch between her legs, hair spread beneath her like a fan, Taj pauses at her outer opening, teasing her with the head, the feeling almost surreal, as he realizes that this is a moment that he's fantasized about his entire adult life.

And now it's a dream that has come true.

His fingers move downward—slowly painting a pathway from her chin to neck, feeling her clavicles and shoulder blades.

Cheyenne reaches around and takes hold of his buttocks, feeling the muscles undulate as she commands him to enter her. And he rushes in, taking her in the way that she longs to be taken, making love to her with abandonment, the weight of his muscular body and his frenzied thrusts boring into her as their bodies hammer the sandy ground.

Taj pummels her as he witnesses his sex being swallowed up, consumed, losing himself inside of her warm wet folds. His arms are thick sinewy muscles that glisten with perspiration; he takes her head in her hands as he presses down, his body covering her as his sweat mingles with hers.

Cheyenne groans.

He feels the vibration deep within the base of her sex—a pitch that is so perfect and pure. Cheyenne is clenching her teeth and squashing her eyes. The feeling is intense.

"Oh God no!" she hisses, "don't make me come yet." She is wriggling underneath him, attempting to slow him down. Her hands are massaging his ass, trying in vain to quell his thrusts. But it does no good.

He tastes her and holds her head firmly between his hands as he thrusts harder, feeling himself expand within her, filling every space that she has to offer.

"Look into my eyes, Jazz," he whispers gently. As her head turns violently away, her teeth clenched, he says, "No . . . look into my eyes. Come with me, Jazz."

The trembling races through her, fingers to hands to arms, descending along her spine to legs that twist and crawl about his waist. The rippling quiver fans out—she feels it deeply and is powerless to stop it. "Oh God, Taj!" she screams, her orgasm at the edge and closing fast, a storm building in intensity before washing over her.

AWAKENING

He holds her face, his eyes inches from her own.

"Look into my eyes," Taj groans, feeling the arc of electricity that stabs at his insides as Cheyenne's entire being shudders. Her body is on fire and trembling out of control.

Cheyenne comes as her mouth opens, breath escaping with a hiss as she melts, staring at those hazel orbs that pulse as his pistons plunge, eyes embracing each other. Taj's entire body freezes as he feels her constrict around him, then suddenly he is a freight train out of control, wheels locked, skidding against the rails as sparks sizzle and fly.

She feels him pulse and strain. He has no choice but to unleash, and he does—willingly, lovingly, his syrup washing into her in spasms. The two lovers are connected—interlocked so tight—their sexes wrapped around each other in an unyielding way; his breath becomes her breath, his spasm her spasm. Cheyenne watches the pulse subside in those hazel eyes; Taj sees it in hers as his hot breath fans over her face and body. When Cheyenne finally returns to earth, she is infused with the awareness of this Christmas gift that is like no other, and closes her eyes as Taj nuzzles against her neck, and buries his face in the cool, delightful sand . . .

Epilogue

Even the change of a dozen seasons cannot quell the remembrance of that Christmas Eve—not for Taj and certainly not for Cheyenne. The particulars are locked away in both of their minds—of that special time that changed them both, forever . . .

There are times, many occasions actually, when either one of them will pause: from taking a sip of pungent coffee, or clinking glasses while in the midst of toasting an excellent bottle of wine, or just waking up from an enjoyable nap, when the senses are not yet honed, but the mind is razor sharp, like Seifu's intimidating blade. The details of that moment come flooding back—lying on a blanket of cooling sand crystals, basking in the shadows of the overhead moon—an invigorating juice racing through their veins as their breathing and heart rates slowly returned to normal, Taj nuzzled against her hot, pulsating neck, his blood-filled member still entombed inside her, like a cocoon, but collapsing, slowly losing signs of life, as the juice of their sex mingled, stirred, like cream poured into black coffee, and became one . . .

It is not the end of a transition that they both reached, together and separately, that marks the end of a new beginning—an inauguration that curls their lips into a smile whenever they consider that night. It's not the particulars of that trip that they remember clearly—coming face-to-face with their demons and making peace with two ends of a wide spectrum—enemies and family, which, with the changing of the seasons, they have grown to share with loved ones. And if those close to them knew the entire unbridled truth of all that transpired between them (which they thankfully do not—some things, as Taj is fond of saying, are better left unsaid), then they might wonder if that romantic Jamaican night represented a new beginning for Taj and Cheyenne, or an ending.

It is, indeed, a question to ask. The answer, however, is not easily forthcoming. For in some ways, that night represented both a beginning for Taj and Cheyenne, and a conclusion.

For when all is said and done, it is that luxurious moment when finally, after so many wanting years, Taj and Cheyenne completed what began for them decades ago—the culmination of much that was left unsaid, the consummation of a lifelong pact, an agreement between eager companions, valiant warriors, fervent lovers, and resolute survivors.

Jamaica was, and always will be, a gathering of souls.

For in the end, that's what Taj and Cheyenne essentially are.

Soul mates.

Always will be, no matter what . . .

Taj raises his glass to toast his wife. Sitting beside him, she is radiant on this particular August evening. They are dining at their favorite restaurant in northwest D.C., an eclectic confluence of hip-hop, art, jazz, and exotic cuisine called *bluespace*, at an upstairs table where they can observe and enjoy the lightshow, away from the piercing din of patrons that frequent this establishment each night— a cozy and romantic spot—perfect for their few close friends.

"Happy anniversary, Baby," Taj says, as their friends clink glasses and nod in her direction. "And, congratulations to the new, *full* professor of American literature at Howard, tenured, I might add!" There is applause at the table as Nicole—her eyes sparkling from a lone candle that catches her pupils just so, creating a fire in her eyes, and a desire stirring in Taj's heart—bows her head demurely.

"You go, girl!" her best friend says, high fiving her as she leans into Nicole, a move predicated on far too much merlot. She drops her voice a notch so as to speak only to Nicole. "And I'm jealous as hell! Damn, you seem to have it all: a wonderful marriage, a great job, a beautiful man," she pauses to take a swig from her wine stem before continuing. "Did I mention a fine man?" she asks incredulously.

"I think you did," Nicole answers warmly, patting her friend's thigh.

Taj strokes his wife's naked arm, tracing a tortuous pattern up her arm as he rises. He leans over and kisses her cheek affectionately as his eye begins to tremor, a metrical quiver that Nicole does not see.

"I'll be back," he says warmly as he brushes a dark hand along his shivering eyelid.

Taj descends the winding stairs and skirts past a throng of tables on the first floor before passing a sleek teakwood bar and heading for the restroom. A minute later he returns, passes the bar again, and slows his step as his gaze sweeps upward to the monitor above the crowded rack of liqueurs and spirits. It is tuned to a local station that is broadcasting the *Billboard* Music Awards, live from Los Angeles.

He pauses and lays his forearms on the bar as his eyes lock on the television. Some well-known Hollywood couple is announcing the nominees for album of the year. Taj feels his pulse quicken when Cheyenne's name is read. His breath catches in his throat as a moment passes.

Then the winner is announced. And Taj witnesses Cheyenne rise majestically from her front-row seat.

Taj returns to the winding stairs with a satisfied smile, content in the knowledge that she has found peace . . .

It is like a dream—she ascends the steps slowly as applause rocks the gigantic room. Light bulbs flash and strobe creating a surreal effect—and Cheyenne wonders if she is living a lie, allowing herself to dream this kind of reverie—but the applause will not cease—it does not falter—it continues to rumble until she raises her hands and gestures for the crowd to quiet.

The silence is deafening.

She takes a breath before beginning.

"Oh my God," she starts, but is forced to pause, yielding to the thunderous claps that reverberate throughout the complex.

"I don't know what to say. This is indeed an honor that I am not worthy to receive."

More applause as she smiles, pressing a palm into her glowing hair.

Cheyenne is radiant in a vibrant red dress that accentuates her bronze hair and cinnamon complexion. It hugs every contour of her body, leaving the crowd—men and women alike—breathless with anticipation.

"There are so many thoughts whirling around in my head right now, because this was a project borne from love, the love of my family, my producers, and my fans—those who coaxed me to go on, to do what I simply and essentially love to do—sing. And so I stand here tonight and give thanks to all of you, my fans, for bestowing this wonderful honor on my first album, *Awakening,* and me.

"There are far too many people to thank—it would take all night. Let me say this—above all, I give thanks to God, for blessing me with a wonderful gift. I thank Him for bringing a savior into my life, a remarkable man who has brought me peace and hope. I give thanks for my beautiful daughter, Ashley, who provides me with strength and unrelenting love each and every day."

At that moment the crowd bursts into more applause and a little girl, no more than a toddler, rises from her seat and skips up the stairs to the podium. The crowd goes wild as Cheyenne bends down to scoop her daughter into her arms.

The young girl wraps her arms tightly around her mother's neck and hugs her before pulling back, gazing into her mother's misty eyes. Cheyenne stares back into those haunting amazing eyes—hazel colored spheres that vibrate with intensity and purity—the calming, almost magical qualities that arrest her every time she gazes upon them.

And in that moment—the crowd disappears. They simply cease to exist—their booming applause fades into background noise like tendrils of smoke that are carried away on wafts of warm air. Only Cheyenne and her daughter are left—eyes locked upon each other, the love of a thousand generations flowing between them.

There is so much to say . . . So many things that she wants to say. So many things she is desperate to convey to her daughter. When the time is right . . .

One day when Ashley is older, Cheyenne is going to take her on a journey to a place far away, where she can tell her a story—the tale of her own journey that began with despair, but ended in triumph, and in peace: peace within herself and with the grandmother Ashley never knew. And when the chronicling of that story is through, Cheyenne will tell her of her father: an amazing man, a great warrior, a best friend, an unfathomable lover, and a soul mate.

Their savior. The one who brought calm to the storm. The one who is responsible for her peace.

"One day, Ashley, you will know," Cheyenne whispers as she blinks back the tears. *One day, baby, I'm going to tell you our story. And then you will know the truth.*

But not tonight . . .

The End
Accokeek, Maryland/
San Francisco, California

In this thrilling debut novel from Carrie H. Johnson, one woman with a dangerous job and a volatile past is feeling the heat from all sides . . .

HOT FLASH

On Sale Now

One

Our bodies arched, both of us reaching for that place of ultimate release we knew was coming. Yes! We screamed at the same time . . . except I kept screaming long after his moment had passed.

You've got to be kidding me, a cramp in my groin? The second time in the three times we had made love. Achieving pretzel positions these days came at a price, but man, how sweet the reward.

"What's the matter, baby? You cramping again?" he asked, looking down at me with genuine concern.

I was pissed, embarrassed, and in pain all at the same time. "Yeah," I answered meekly, grimacing.

"It's okay. It's okay, sugar," he said, sliding off me. He reached out and pulled me into the curvature of his body, leaving the wet spot to its own demise. I settled in. Gently, he massaged my thigh. His hands soothed me. Little by little, the cramp went away. Just as I dozed off, my cell phone rang.

"Mph, mph, mph," I muttered. "Never a moment's peace."

Calvin stirred. "Huh?"

"Nothin', baby, shhhh," I whispered, easing from his grasp and reaching for the phone from the bedside table. As quietly as I could, I answered the phone the same way I always did.

"Muriel Mabley."

"Did I get you at a bad time, partner?" Laughton chuckled. He used the same line whenever he called. He never thought twice about waking me, no matter the hour. I worked to live and lived to work—at least that's been my story for twenty years, the last seventeen as a firearms forensics expert for the Philadelphia Police Department. I had the dubious distinction of being the first woman in the unit and one of two minorities. The other was my partner, Laughton McNair.

At forty-nine, I was beginning to think I was blocking the blessing God intended for me. I felt like I had blown past any hope of a true love in pursuit of a damn suspect.

"You there?" Laughton said, laughing louder.

"Hee hee, hell. I finally find someone and

you runnin' my ass ragged, like you don't even want it to last. What now?" I said.

"Speak up. I can hardly hear you."

"I said . . . "

"I heard you." More chuckles from Laughton. "You might want to rethink a relationship. Word is we've got another dead wife and again the husband swears he didn't do it. Says she offed herself. That makes three dead wives in three weeks. Hell, must be the season or something in the water."

Not wanting to move much or turn the light on, I let my fingers search blindly through my bag on the nightstand until they landed on paper and a pen. Pulling my hand out of my bag with paper and pen was another story. I knocked over the half-filled champagne glass also on the nightstand. "Damn it!" I was like a freaking circus act, trying to save the paper, keep the bubbly from getting on the bed, stop the glass from breaking, and keep from dropping the phone.

"Sounds like you're fighting a war over there," Laughton said.

"Just give me the address."

"If you can't get away . . . "

"Laughton, just . . . "

"You don't have to yell."

He let a moment of silence pass before he said, "Thirteen ninety-one Berkhoff. I'll meet you there."

"I'm coming," I said and clicked off.

"You okay?" Calvin reached out to recapture me. I let him and fell back into the warmth of his embrace. Then I caught myself, sat up, and clicked the light on—but not without a sigh of protest.

Calvin rose. He rested his head in his palm and flashed that gorgeous smile at me. "Can't blame a guy for trying," he said.

"It's a pity I can't do you any more lovin' right now. I can't sugarcoat it. This is my life," I complained on my way to the bathroom.

"So you keep telling me."

I felt uptight about leaving Calvin in the house alone. My son, Travis, would be home from college in the morning, his first spring break from Lincoln University. He and Calvin had not met. In all the years before this night, I had not brought a man home, except Laughton, and at least a decade had passed since I'd had any form of a romantic relationship. The memory chip filled with that information had almost disintegrated. Then along came Calvin.

When I came out, Calvin was up and dressed. He was five foot ten, two hundred pounds of muscle, the kind of muscle that flexed at his slightest move. Pure lovely. He pulled me close and pressed his wet lips to mine. His breath, mixed with a hint of citrus from his cologne, made every nerve in my body pulsate.

"Next time we'll do my place. You can sing

to me while I make you dinner," he whispered. "Soft, slow melodies." He crooned, "You Must Be a Special Lady," as he rocked me back and forth, slow and steady. His gooey caramel voice touched my every nerve ending, head to toe. Calvin is a singer and owns a nightclub, which is how we met. I was at his club with friends and Calvin and I—or rather, Calvin and my alter ego, spurred on by my friends, of course— entertained the crowd with duets all night.

He held me snugly against his chest and buried his face in the hollow of my neck while brushing his fingertips down the length of my body.

"Mmm . . . sounds luscious," was all I could muster.

The Interstate was dark, unusual no matter what time, day or night.

In the darkness, I could easily picture Calvin's face, bright with a satisfied smile. I could still feel his hot breath on my neck, the soft strumming of his fingers on my back. I had it bad. Butterflies reached down to my navel and made me shiver. I felt like I was nineteen again, first love or some such foolishness.

Flashing lights from an oncoming police car brought my thoughts around to what was ahead, a possible suicide. How anyone could think life was so bad that they would kill themselves never settled with me. Life's stuff enters pit territory sometimes, but then tomorrow comes and anything is possible again. Of course, the idea that the husband could be the killer could take one even deeper into pit territory. The man you once loved, who made you scream during lovemaking, now not only wants you gone, moved out, but dead.

When I rounded the corner to Berkhoff Street, the scene was chaotic, like the trappings of a major crime. I pulled curbside and rolled to a stop behind a news truck. After I turned off Bertha, my 2000 Saab gray convertible, she rattled in protest for a few moments before going quiet. As I got out, local news anchor Sheridan Meriwether hustled from the front of the news truck and shoved a microphone in my face before I could shut the car door.

"Back off, Sheridan. You'll know when we know," I told her.

"True, it's a suicide?" Sheridan persisted.

"If you know that, then why the attack? You know we don't give out information in suicides."

"Confirmation. Especially since two other wives have been killed in the past few weeks."

"Won't be for a while. Not tonight anyway."

"Thanks, Muriel." She nodded toward Bertha. "Time you gave the old gray lady a permanent rest, don't you think?"

"Hey, she's dependable."

She chuckled her way back to the front of the news truck. Sheridan was the only newsperson I would give the time of day. We went back two decades, to rookie days when my mom and dad were killed in a car crash. Sheridan and several other newspeople had accompanied the police to inform me. She returned the next day, too, after the buzz had faded. A drunk driver sped through a red light and rammed my parents' car head-on. That was the story the police told the papers. The driver of the other car cooked to a crisp when his car exploded after hitting my parents' car, then a brick wall. My parents were on their way home from an Earth, Wind & Fire concert at the Tower Theater.

Sheridan produced a series on drunk drivers in Philadelphia, how their indiscretions affected families and children on both sides of the equation, which led to a national broadcast. Philadelphia police cracked down on drunk drivers and legislation passed with compulsory loss of licenses. Several other cities and states followed suit.

I showed my badge to the young cop guarding the front door and entered the small foyer. In front of me was a white-carpeted staircase. To the left was the living room. Laughton, his expression stonier than I expected, stood next to the detective questioning who I supposed was the husband. He sat on the couch, leaned forward with his elbows resting on his thighs, his head hanging down. Two girls clad in *Frozen* pajamas huddled next to him on the couch, one on either side.

The detective glanced at me, then back at the man. "Where were you?"

"I just got here, man," the man said. "Went upstairs and found her on the floor."

"And the kids?"

"My daughter spent the night with me. She had a sleepover at my house. This is Jeanne, lives a few blocks over. She got homesick and wouldn't stop crying, so I was bringing them back here. Marcy and I separated, but we're trying to work things out." He choked up, unable to speak any more.

"At three a.m."

"I told you, the child was having a fit. Wanted her mother."

A tank of a woman charged through the front door, "Oh my God. Baby, are you all right?" She pushed past the police officer there and clomped across the room, sending those close to look for cover. The red-striped flannel robe she wore and pink furry slippers, size thirteen at least, made her look like a giant candy cane with feet.

"Wade, what the hell is happenin' here?" She moved in and lifted the girl from the sofa by her arm. Without giving him a chance to answer, she continued, "C'mon, baby. You're coming with me."

An officer stepped sideways and blocked the way. "Ma'am, you can't take her—"

The woman's head snapped around like the devil possessed her, ready to spit out nasty words followed by green fluids. She never stopped stepping.

I expect she would have trampled the officer, but Laughton interceded. "It's all right, Jackson. Let her go," he said.

Jackson sidestepped out of the woman's way before Laughton's words settled.

Laughton nodded his head in my direction. "Body's upstairs."

The house was spotless. White was the color: white furniture, white walls, white drapes, white wall-to-wall carpet, white picture frames. The only real color came in the mass of throw pillows that adorned the couch and a wash of plants positioned around the room.

I went upstairs and headed to the right of the landing, into a bedroom where an officer I knew, Mark Hutchinson, was photographing the scene. Body funk permeated the air. I wrinkled my nose.

"Hey, M&M," Hutchinson said.

"That's Muriel to you." I hated when my colleagues took the liberty to call me that.

Sometimes I wanted to nail Laughton with a front kick to the groin for starting the nickname.

He shook his head. "Ain't me or the victim. She smells like a violet." He tilted his head back, sniffed, and smiled.

Hutchinson waved his hand in another direction. "I'm about done here."

I stopped at the threshold of the bathroom and perused the scene. Marcy Taylor lay on the bathroom floor. A small hole in her temple still oozed blood. Her right arm was extended over her head, and she had a .22 pistol in that hand. Her fingernails and toenails looked freshly painted. When I bent over her body, the sulfur-like smell of hair relaxer backed me up a bit. Her hair was bone-straight. The white silk gown she wore flowed around her body as though staged. Her cocoa brown complexion looked ashen with a pasty, white film.

"Shame," Laughton said to my back. "She was a beautiful woman." I jerked around to see him standing in the doorway.

"Check this out," I said, pointing to the lay of the nightgown over the floor.

"I already did the scene. We'll talk later," he said.

"Damn it, Laughton. Come here and check this out." But when I turned my head, he was gone.

I finished checking out the scene and went outside for some fresh air. Laughton was on the front lawn talking to an officer. He beelined for his car when he saw me.

"What the hell is wrong with you?" I muttered, jogging to catch up with him. Louder. "Laughton, what the hell—"

He dropped anchor. Caught off guard, I plowed into him. He waited until I peeled myself off him and regained my footing, then said, "Nothing. Wade says they separated a few months ago and were trying to get it together, so he came over for some making up. He used his key to enter and found her dead on the bathroom floor."

"No, he said he was bringing the little girl home because she was homesick."

"Yeah, well, then you heard it all."

He about-faced.

I grabbed his arm and attempted to spin him around. "You act like you know this one or something," I practically screeched at him.

"I do."

I cringed and softened my tone five octaves at least when I managed to speak again. "How?"

"I was married to her . . . a long time ago."

He might as well have backhanded me upside the head. "You never—"

"I have an errand to run. I'll see you back at the lab."

I stared after him long after he got in his car and sped off.

The sun was rising by the time the scene was secured: body and evidence bagged, husband and daughter gone back home. It spewed warm tropical hues over the city. By the time I reached the station, the hues had turned cold metallic gray. I pulled into a parking spot and answered the persistent ring of my cell phone. It was Nareece.

"Hey, sis. My babies got you up this early?" I said, feigning a light mood. My babies were Nareece's eight-year-old twin daughters.

Nareece groaned. "No. Everyone's still sleeping."

"You should be, too."

"Couldn't sleep."

"Oh, so you figured you'd wake me up at this ungodly hour in the morning. Sure, why not? We're talkin' sisterly love here, right?" I said. We chuckled. "I've been up since three anyway, working a case." I waited for her to say something, but she stayed silent. "Reece?" More silence. "C'mon, Reecey, we've been through this so many times. Please don't tell me you're trippin' again."

"A bell goes off in my head every time this date rolls around. I believe I'll die with it going off," Nareece confessed.

"Therapy isn't helping?"

"You mean the shrink? She ain't worth the paper she prints her bills on. I get more from talking to you every day. It's all you, Muriel. What would I do without you?"

"I'd say we've helped each other through, Reecey."

Silence filled the space again. Meanwhile, Laughton pulled his Audi Quattro in next to my Bertha and got out. I knocked on the window to get his attention. He glanced in my direction and moved on with his gangster swagger as though he didn't see me.

"I have to go to work, Reece. I just pulled into the parking lot after being at a scene."

"Okay."

"Reece, you've got a great husband, two beautiful daughters, and a gorgeous home, baby. Concentrate on all that and quit lookin' behind you."

Nareece and John had ten years of marriage. John is Vietnamese. The twins were striking, inheritors of almond-shaped eyes, "good" curly black hair, and amber skin. Rose and Helen, named after our mother and grandmother. John balked at their names because they did not reflect his heritage. But he was mush where Nareece was concerned.

"You're right. I'm good except for two days out of the year, today and on Travis's birthday. And you're probably tired of hearing me."

"I'll listen as long as you need me to. It's you and me, Reecey. Always has been, always will be. I'll call you back later today. I promise."

I clicked off and stayed put for a few minutes, bogged down by the realization of Reece's growing obsession with my son, way more than in past years, which conjured up ugly scenes for me. I prayed for a quick passing, though a hint of guilt pierced my gut. Did I pray for her sake, my sake, or Travis's? What scared me anyway?

Kiki Swinson, the bestselling author known for "fast, tension-packed" (Library Journal) novels featuring the glamour and grit of Virginia's most notorious streets, shows what happens when a criminal partnership takes a detour that puts its members on the road to jealousy, revenge, and murder . . .

THE SCORE

On Sale Now

One

Lauren

My feet moved at the speed of lightning. I could feel the wind beating on my skin so hard it made snot wet the inside of my nostrils. My entire body was covered with a thick sheen of sweat and I could feel it burning my armpits. My breath escaped my mouth in jagged, raggedy puffs and my chest burned. My heart felt like it would burst through the front of it. Even feeling as terrible as I did, I would not and could not stop moving.

"Move!"

"Get out of my fucking way!"

"Watch out!"

"Move!"

I screamed command after command at the

nosy-ass people who were staring and gawking and being in my damn way. My legs were moving like those of a swift and agile cheetah as I swerved and swayed through the throngs of people on Virginia Beach Boulevard. I was met by more than one mouthful of gasps and groans and I could faintly see more than one wide-eyed, mouth-agape stare as people gawked at me like I was a crazy woman. I guess I did look crazy running through the high-end shopping area with no shoes on. I had run straight out my Louboutins, my expensive embellished Balmain skirt was hitched up around my hips, my vixen weave was blowing in the wind, and my Chanel caviar bag was strapped around my arm like a slave chain. I could feel that my makeup was a cakey, smudged mess all over my face and eyes. But I didn't give a damn. I wasn't going to stop running. No matter what. Looking crazy was the least of my worries.

I had run track in high school and it was still paying off now, but clearly I wasn't in the same athletic shape. Still, I wasn't about to go out like this. I wasn't going to get captured on the street and probably murdered for something that wasn't totally my fault. I had been pushed and provoked to do everything that I did. All of the mistakes. All of the grimy shit I had done over the years. All of it was because

I was born at a disadvantage from day fucking one.

I didn't want to die. I had always seen myself growing old with a few kids and grandkids surrounding me when I was ready to be settled. I would've given anything to be old and settled at this moment. But, of course, life threw me a curveball.

I could hear the thunderous footfalls of the three men chasing me. If they weren't so damn gorilla big and slower than me they would have caught me by now.

"Hey! Are you okay?" I heard a man on the street yell at me as I flew past him, nearly knocking him over. Why the hell was he asking me such a dumb question when you could clearly see that I was being chased by three hulking goons dressed in all black with their guns probably showing on their waists or maybe even in their hands. Thank goodness I am always so alert or they would've walked right up on me while I unsuspectingly ate my lunch at the posh restaurant and grabbed me. It was the fact that I had only been back in town for a few hours, the disappearance of my lunch companion, and the suspicious looks that had alerted me in the first place. How could I have been so trusting? So naïve and stupid, too.

I could feel the look of terror contorting

my face, so I know damn well passersby could see the fear etched on every inch of it.

Finally, I dipped through a side alley and the first door I tried allowed me inside. Thank God! With my chest heaving up and down I rested my back against another cold metal door inside and slid down to the floor. My legs were still trembling and my muscles were on fire in places on my body I didn't even know existed. I tried to slow down my rapid breathing so I could hear whether the men had noticed me dipping into the alley but the more I tried to calm myself the more reality set in about the grave danger I was in. I was probably about to be murdered or worse, tortured and then murdered right in a dank alleyway in the place I thought I would never return to. If I hadn't gotten that call, it would have been years before I crept back here. I thought about Matt and wondered if he was the one who had sent these men after me. But how would he have known I was back? I knew Matt had a lot of selfish ways about him and although shit had gone south with us, I never thought he would try to do something like this to me. I expected that if he wanted to confront me, he would come himself. Even if it was Yancy who had sent the goons, I would think Matt would have tried to spare me.

CLANG!

A loud noise outside interrupted my thoughts and caused me to jump. I clasped both of my hands over my mouth and forced the scream that had crept up my throat back down. Sweat trickled down my face and burned my eyes. My heart jackhammered against my chest bone so hard it actually hurt. My stomach knotted up so tightly the cramps were almost unbearable. I dropped my head. Suddenly I felt like vomiting.

"I don't see her! She's not down here!" I heard one of the goons outside of the door scream to the others. I swallowed hard and started praying under my breath.

Dear God, I am sorry for all of the things I've done. I don't know how things got so far gone. I never meant anything by any of it. I just wanted to live a better life than I had as a child. I guess with the mother you gave me and the hand you dealt me, I should've just handled it. I should've worked harder and not try to take the easy way out all of the time. I knew stealing is wrong. Since the first time I stole a credit card from my foster mother's purse, I'd known it was wrong. But I got addicted to the feeling that I'd gotten over on someone. I felt powerful. I remember the times I'd hear her talking to my foster father about some of the fraud scams she witnessed by working as a bank manager. It was interesting to hear how bank and credit card frauds were being committed on a daily basis. It all seemed too easy, too intoxicating. I had to test the waters. . . .

So here I am today. I'm literally running for my life. Maybe this is your way of teaching me a lesson. Trust me, I hear you loud and clear. If you let me get out of this, I swear I will change my life. I don't even know how things got this far . . .